One-of-a-Kind Bride

One-of-a-Kind Bride

Charlene Sands

One-of-a-Kind Bride

Tule Publishing First Printing, April 2020

The Tule Publishing, Inc.

First Publication by Tule Publishing 2020

Cover design by Elizabeth Mackey

ISBN: 978-1-951786-17-5

Dedication

For Everley, Kyra, Madyson and Lila,
our four sweet girls. You are my inspiration.
Love you to the moon and back!
This one's especially for you!

Prologue

TAYLOR PRESTON RAN up the gazebo steps, the Texas sun warming her cheeks. "Come on, Coop. It's time to play restaurant. And this time I'm the waitress and you're the customer." She picked up her pencil and pad and waited. "Aren't you coming?"

Coop's mouth twisted like he just ate a sour lemon. "That's a girlie game. Let's play pirates. I'm the captain." He sliced the air with his pretend sword and Taylor folded her arms across her chest.

"We played that yesterday and the day before that."

He scratched his head. "I know, but I don't like your game much."

"But, Coop, you promised me."

Her cousin Julie walked up. "That's right, you promised her."

"No, I didn't."

"You did so," Taylor said. "And you know it. Mama says it's not right breaking your promise. She says you shouldn't make a promise you can't keep. Right, Julie?"

"That's right and Taylor never breaks her promises."

Taylor was glad her cousin stuck up for her. Julie, Ryan "Coop" Cooper and she were nine years old. She always spent her summers here, playing games with Julie and Coop and swimming in Aunt Suzie's pool. But Taylor only had one day left before she had to leave Last Stand and go back to school in New York with her mother.

Coop stood tall and put his lips together like a stubborn old mule. Even like that, she thought he was cute with pretty blue eyes and shaggy brown hair, but she'd never tell him that. No, that would be horrible.

"No fair," he said, glancing at her and Julie. "It's two against one."

"But we play your games a lot more than you play ours, so it is fair," Taylor pointed out.

Finally, Coop grumbled and stomped up the gazebo steps. "Okay, fine. We'll play restaurant."

Taylor beamed inside. "Thanks, Coop. I'm glad you kept your promise."

He shook his head. "Promises are silly."

"No, they're not. They're important. If you give your word to someone, you should keep it."

"Are we gonna play or what?"

"Play."

A few minutes later, Aunt Suzie called Julie into the house. It was Julie's turn to pour the lemonade and bring it out. Aunt Suzie would bring out cookies. She and Coop stopped playing to wait for their treats.

Taylor fiddled around with the notepad, making ink swirls and thinking. "You know how you say promises are silly? They're not. They can be fun. I play a promise game with my mama sometimes."

"What game?"

"You make me a promise. I make you a promise. We write it down and then see who kept their promise."

He lifted a shoulder. "Sounds okay."

"Okay? It's gonna be fun. Why don't we make a promise to each other right now and next summer when I come back, we can see who kept theirs."

Coop's face lit up. "You mean, if I ask you to promise to eat a bug, you'll do it?"

"Eww, no. Not like that. What if I promised to...to try to get good grades in math?"

"That sounds boring. What if you promised to eat peanut butter and jelly sandwiches once a week?"

She scrunched up her nose. "I don't like peanut butter."

He smiled. "I know. Maybe you would if you tried it more."

"If I say yes, what's your promise to me?"

"Um...what if I...uh, make you something from my dad's shop? Something out of wood?"

"You'd promise that? What would you make?"

"I promise to make you a...a little treasure box."

"Really? Wow! I'll write these down." She would love that. Taylor picked up her pen and wrote out the promises on two pieces of paper. "All done. Thanks, Coop."

"Hey, wait a minute. How am I going to know if you kept your promise to me?"

"I'll send you pictures and then when I come back next summer, you can ask my mother." Taylor rolled up the two papers. She wasn't happy about having to eat peanut butter. Yuck. But once a week wasn't so bad, and Coop didn't say how *much* peanut butter had to be in the sandwich. "Let's hide them under the gazebo."

Coop grabbed the papers and ran down the steps first. He searched for a place at the back of the gazebo. "This board is loose," he said, wiggling the wood free. "We can put the papers under here. It's a good spot."

"Yeah, nobody will ever find them here."

Coop tossed the two papers inside, under the gazebo floor, and then put the board back in place. He rose and smiled at her. She smiled back. She was glad Cooper wanted to play this promise game.

It made going home a little easier.

She was going to miss Last Stand.

And Coop and Julie most of all.

Chapter One

THIS WAS THE biggest day in Taylor's life, in recent memory that was.

And the morning called for coffee. She crossed the street, fighting heavy winds, one hand clutching her oversized design briefcase, the other reaching for Coffee Corner's doorknob. New York never did anything on a small scale so when a gigantic gust pushed her inside the coffee house she hung on for dear life and came to a quick stop when the door closed behind her. It was warm inside and homey, the aroma of freshly brewed coffee helping to calm her nerves.

"Look what the wind blew in," Melanie said from behind the counter, her smile wide.

"Literally, right? I thought it was supposed to be spring."

"Apparently, the Big Apple didn't get the memo. So, today's the day, Taylor. Are you excited?"

"*Jittery* is a better word." Taylor removed her coat, set down her briefcase and shook out her hair. This morning she'd spiral curled it and spent extra time with her makeup, hoping to make a good impression with the design executives at Boutique Bridal. Too bad downtown weather wasn't cooperating. The wind had gobbled up her curls and spit the strands out into an unruly mess.

"Well, I've got your sustenance ready. Two hot vanilla lattes and sweet treats."

"The cinnamon rolls look amazing, but I think I'm too nervous to eat." She grabbed one of the lattes and wrapped her hand around the cup. Soothing heat seeped into her fingers as she blew away steam and took a sip.

"Take them to Simone along with her latte," Mel said. "And your other coworkers. On me. To celebrate your new designs."

"That's sweet of you, Mel. But I can't—"

"Tut, tut, tut," Mel said, her polite way of shutting her up. "You can. And you will." She shrugged. "That's what you get for being my best customer and friend. You didn't abandon me when they built that giant-sized coffeehouse that shall remain nameless across the street."

"I promised you, didn't I? Besides your coffee is better and so are your pastries."

"Your promise goes a long way. Don't think I don't know that you've sent customers my way. I really appreciate it, Taylor. More than you know."

Melanie's business had dropped off by fifty percent when the competition opened its doors.

Taylor had given her a promise and she'd been supporting her coffee shop ever since. "You deserve it."

"And you deserve to have your new line of bridal gowns

approved. Your talent needs to be recognized."

One could only hope. She'd gone to design college for four years, studied in Italy for two summers and had worked in retail bridal shops until she'd landed this job. Her first line of bridal gowns had made a decent showing, but that was when Eric Banning Junior, the son of the owner, had been her boss. He'd loved her edgy designs. Now, Eric Senior was at the helm again and he'd told her to do what she did best. And she had. She'd developed a new line of gowns, putting her heart and soul in her work. Now, all her eggs were in one basket. And she hoped it was enough.

"Thanks for your support," she told Mel.

Mel nodded. "Hey, why don't you have a seat and drink your coffee. I'll package all this up for you. Maybe you'll get your appetite back when the execs gush all over your designs." Mel gave her a friendly wink, and Taylor smiled.

"Sounds good, Mel."

She sat at a café table finishing off her coffee and glanced at the clock. She had half an hour until her meeting. The butterflies in her stomach took flight again. She squeezed her eyes closed and her mama's image flashed in her mind. Tall and pretty, with a quirky sense of humor and a gift of always saying the right thing, her mama's wise words were always close, always a part of her. "Go after your dreams, Taylor. If you want to design gowns, then do it and be happy in your decision."

And she'd vowed to her mama she would. "I'll be successful, Mama. I promise you."

Her mother had smiled then. Because she knew Taylor never broke her promises.

TAYLOR STEPPED INTO the conference room at precisely nine a.m. and held her breath as she stared into Mr. Banning's unreadable eyes. He stood up as she walked in, a lost art for many men, but Banning Senior, as they called him at the office, was always a gentleman.

"Good morning, Taylor. Have a seat."

She hesitated a second, scanning the empty room. Where were all the associates? Were they running late? She took a seat adjacent to the boss at the long conference table. She gulped quietly. It was daunting seeing her beloved designs displayed on the overhead screen. She was proud of her work, had spent months and months on these designs, trying to come up with something unique and true to her own vision, while also keeping with the Boutique Bridal brand.

"How are you this morning, Taylor?" he asked.

"I'm fine. A bit nervous."

"Would you like some coffee?"

"Thank you, but I've already had a cup." Melanie's coffee was churning in her stomach now.

Something was off, way off.

"Well then, let's get right to the point. Your work is very

well done. You have talent, Miss Preston, and we've enjoyed having you as part of our team, but—"

There was always a *but* and she was afraid this one would change her life, no…it would destroy her life.

She mustered up the courage to ask, "But?"

"I'm sorry to say, it's not for us, Taylor. The work is, well, too unconventional for our brand. We have to meet client expectations, and though your designs are valuable and well done, they don't scream Boutique Bridal. In fact, just the opposite. We were looking for something…"

"Unique, was what I was told. The line should reflect something a bit different. That's what I brought you."

"Ah, yes. I can see how you might think that. But I'm afraid we've decided to take a more traditional route. We like soft curves and detailed lines and what you've given us here are sharp points and jagged edges."

"I can make adjustments to the line if—"

"I don't think so, Taylor. We've already given you two chances at this. And I don't want to stifle your creative talent."

"But Eric Junior liked the first line I presented and the sales were good."

"Yes, that's true. But my son took some liberties with our brand and I had to return to the company get us back on track. I'm afraid your creative input is not part of the equation."

"So, you're…firing me?" The words trailed off, her heart

totally shattered.

"We're letting you go, to pursue your talent elsewhere." He rose from his seat. "Take as much time as you need to get your things in order. It was a pleasure having you at Boutique and I wish you the best of luck. Goodbye, Taylor." He put out his hand and gave her a look that said *no hard feelings*.

Only she had them. In a major way. Her feelings were hurt. She hadn't given him jagged edges or sharp points. She'd given him contemporary style, designs that appealed to the current day bride.

She shook his hand. "Thank you, Mr. Banning."

He gave her a final nod and walked out of the room, leaving her and her nine new designs behind.

She sat there numb. Minutes rolled by and then there was a knock at the door and Simone walked in. She didn't say a word. She sat down next to her and grabbed her hand. Simone was the best; they'd been immediate friends from day one. She worked in human resources.

"You heard."

"I'm sorry. Mr. Banning came in to tell me. For what it's worth, he feels badly."

"Yet, he still let me go. I was told they wanted something different. Something unique. And they had faith in me to deliver. But they really didn't want different. They wanted different, *but the same*. I guess I was a fool for not understanding the code."

"You're no fool, Taylor. You're a major talent. Those designs are amazing. And I'm not just saying it to make you feel better. If I ever get married, I'd wear any one of your gowns with pride."

She stacked her hand over Simone's, a layer of friendship that she needed right now. "Thanks."

"What can I do to help?" she asked.

"You're doing it." She gave Simone a wobbly smile. It was all she could manage. "I'll be…okay. I guess."

"Why don't I come over with dinner tonight? We'll have pizza and watch an old movie."

"Thanks, Simone. But I'll take a rain check. I have to figure out…my life."

"Well, yes you do. And you will. But you don't have to do it tonight. And you don't have to do it alone."

"I guess not. But, suddenly, I'm feeling closed in. Like I need to run. Like I need to get away from New York." The feeling shocked her.

She'd always thought of the city as her home, her haven and her sanctuary, but right now, claws of indecision, confusion and injury were pawing at her. She'd failed before, but not like this. Not enough to lose her job.

Simone's dark eyes went soft, not with pity but with understanding. She'd had a romance go bad, and the breakup had been devastating. Rejection was rejection and it damn well hurt. Simone had left town, needing a change of pace, needing to recharge her batteries and gain perspective. She'd visited her folks in Atlanta, her hometown, and she'd come back with a better attitude, ready to take on the world again. The only problem for Taylor was that she *was* home. New York was where she lived and, up until an hour ago, where she worked. She'd grown up here.

"Didn't you just finish designing your cousin's wedding dress?" she asked.

Taylor nodded, not seeing the relevance to the conversation.

"Isn't that wedding coming up?"

"Not until next month."

"So, why not visit your cousin Julie a little early? She lives in that small town, doesn't she? And you're always saying how much you miss her. She's been like a sister to you and you're the same age and—"

"Simone, you're on a roll, but I can't just barge in on Julie's life. I was planning to go one week before the wedding."

"So, now you go a few weeks early. I'm sure your cousin would love to have your help with the wedding plans."

"I don't know. I'd be lousy company. I wouldn't want to bring Julie down."

"Well, I'm no expert, but if you give yourself a few days to grieve over your designs, then head out, I can almost guarantee you, you'll have a good time and come back in a much better frame of mind."

"You think?"

Simone nodded. "I think."

Taylor let out a deep breath. The idea had merit and she did have wonderful times in Last Stand when she was younger. She'd love to spend extra time with Julie and get to know her fiancé a little better. Miguel wasn't originally from Last Stand, but he'd fallen hard for Julie and picked up stakes, figuring he could move his online tech support business anywhere.

That kind of love was hard to find. An image flashed of Coop, the seventeen-year-old boy she'd left behind in Last Stand to pursue her dreams. They'd grown up being childhood friends, but on that last summer together, they'd fallen head over heels in love. It had been the best summer of her life, one that she'd tucked way back in her memory. *Puppy love* was how her mother had defined it and Taylor knew that to be true. She had lofty dreams that no one guy could keep down, but Ryan "Coop" Cooper wasn't easily forgotten. Even after twelve years, she still thought of him and hoped he was happy.

"You know, your idea is growing on me," she told Simone.

"Like a weed or a fresh blooming flower?"

She chuckled, something she didn't think she'd do after being fired by one of the most prestigious bridal corporations in the country. "Maybe a little bit of both. Sort of an unwanted wildflower that is pretty enough to catch the eye."

"I'll take that. So, dinner is on, right? Pizza, M&Ms and

popcorn. We'll rent your favorite movie." Which was *The Devil Wears Prada*. No, that wouldn't do. She didn't need reminders of her failure in life. She'd find something to watch that didn't involve fashion. Maybe a movie about a dog or something.

"Right. Okay." Taylor turned to hug her best bud, squeezing her extra tight. "I don't know what I'd do without you, Simone."

Her friend didn't know it yet, but she'd just saved Taylor from having a soul-searching, heart-wrenching, tears-flowing, pity-party horrible night. Correction, Simone did so know it. Taylor saw the truth on her expression. Simone wanted to come to her rescue, the way Taylor had when Simone's jerk-face boyfriend had dumped her.

"Right back at ya," Simone said.

And Taylor was grateful for the rescue.

Even if it was for just one night.

THEY SETTLED ON *The Notebook*. So not a dog movie, but it was a far cry from fashion and just what Taylor needed. She loved the time period and flashbacks and, honestly, she could look at Ryan Gosling for hours. She ate three pieces of pepperoni pizza and half a giant-sized bag of M&Ms. Her stomach was a battlefield now, acid fighting against sugar and the warfare was grueling. But at least for the last three hours since Simone showed up with the goodies, she hadn't thought too much about losing her job, or her next career move.

She'd called Julie this afternoon and they'd spoken for over an hour, her cousin a good listener and before Taylor could even broach the subject of showing up in Last Stand early, Julie had invited her. "You have to come. I'd love to have your help and it would do you a world of good to get out of the city. Please promise me that you'll come as soon as possible."

And Taylor had promised. Just like that, her immediate future was planned out. She'd be leaving on a flight for Texas day after tomorrow and luckily, she was able to change her reservation without it costing a major fortune.

The movie ended and Simone was crying. Taylor's eyes had misted up too. She rose to grab a box of tissues and handed her friend one.

"It gets me every time."

"And yet, we keep watching it."

"Yeah, it's that good," Simone said. After she dried her eyes, she glanced up. "How're you doing? You've been quiet."

"Busy eating away my grief. I did major damage on the M&Ms. The sugar is bouncing off the walls inside giving me tummy rolls."

"Tummy rolls? Is that a thing?"

"You know, when you're doing dips on a rollercoaster, or

when you're driving and speed up on the down side of a hill and your stomach rolls. That's what mine feels like right now."

"O-kay," she said, her brows gathering. "Sorry."

"It's my own fault. I ate too much and I'm paying the price right now."

"You don't want to get sick before your trip," Simone said.

"I won't. But you have to admit, this day has been kind of horrendous. You know what I mean?"

"Of course I do, but I have to tell ya, you're handling it pretty well."

"That's because you're here with me. Otherwise, I'd be falling apart."

Simone rose, grabbing the empty pizza box and paper plates. "Then I'm glad I'm here."

She walked the stuff over to the trash and dumped it in. "Before I go," she said, "I'd love to see your cousin's dress."

"And I'd love to show it to you. Follow me," she said. She led Simone into her bedroom, where the gossamer wedding dress—well, the bare bones of the dress—was hanging high up on the wall. "It's definitely a work in progress."

"I'm just amazed you can work on it from across the country."

"I lucked out. Julie and I are the same size. When she sent me her measurements, they were almost identical to mine. So, it's been easier than I thought it would be. I've been putting it on and checking my work firsthand."

"Now, I'm more impressed."

"There's more beading to do."

"All hand stitched."

"Yes, and the hideaway zipper's going to be a challenge, but it's the detailing that's going to make this gown come to life."

"Julie's a lucky girl."

"We'll see."

Simone gave her a don't-go-there look. "She's going to love it, because you're great at what you do. Don't doubt yourself, Taylor. Ever."

Simone was not only a loyal friend, she was a big fan of her work, which warmed her inside, but Taylor still couldn't believe she was out of a job. She'd worked so hard to get to this position in life and now, it all seemed to have blown away on a frivolous gust. She felt like the star of a terrible dream. She wanted to wake up and have it all go away. She wanted her old reality, not this new one that totally sucked.

She said goodbye to Simone, giving her a long, loving embrace. It was late and her friend had to get up early for work the next morning. Whereas tomorrow, Taylor had only to pack her bags and lament her future.

She donned her blue polka dot pajamas, which were much too cheery for her mood, and slipped into bed after midnight. Oddly, as her eyes closed, the first image filling her head was of a seventeen-year-old Ryan Cooper, kissing her goodbye for the final time behind Julie's gazebo in Last Stand.

Chapter Two

AS SOON AS she landed at the Texas airport and caught sight of Julie's smiling face, Taylor's entire body relaxed. The air here was fresher, and warmer than the cold, almost nonexistent spring in New York, and now a deep sense of déjà vu set in, recalling the excitement of visiting Julie as a child. Their summers together, she, Julie, and Coop were the best and they'd nicknamed themselves the Three Musketeers. Coop didn't mind playing with girls; he was the most vocal and often dictated the terms.

"Julie, it's great to see you." She hugged her cousin tightly. Even though it'd been two years since she'd come to New York for a visit, it was like no time had actually passed between them. They spoke on the phone regularly and FaceTimed often.

"Same here. Oh, we're going to have a good time, Taye. But first," Julie said, taking her hands and giving them a loving squeeze, "tell me, how're you doing? I'm so sorry about the way things turned out at Boutique Bridal. I swear, they don't know what they're missing."

"Thanks, hon. I'll be okay." She shrugged. "Dad says one

day I'll be glad about this. He says I'll find a place where I'm really appreciated. You know, he's a great believer in destiny."

"I know. How's he doing?"

"Going strong. But I still worry about him doing too much at his age." Her father was a minister and had been living and preaching to his congregation in Florida ever since her mom had passed some five years ago. Knowing him, he hadn't taken a day off since.

"Still thinks he's thirty-nine and holding?" Julie asked.

"Exactly." Her dad was thirty years older than that. "But he's excited to officiate your wedding."

"I can't wait to see Uncle Jay. It's been too long."

They retrieved her luggage and the garment bag housing Julie's wedding gown and off they went, her cousin behind the wheel of a red convertible sports car. Funny thing, ever since Julie had met Miguel, the grade school teacher in her had become much more adventurous and less timid about things. Love, she'd said, had a way of changing a person. But love had eluded Taylor all these years.

Unless she counted that last summer with Coop. They'd been so young, with both of their lives ahead of them. And she'd had to leave. She'd had a promise to keep. To her mom and to herself.

As they motored toward Julie's farmhouse on the outskirts of Last Stand, they reminisced about their youth and all the changes occurring lately in town. The car was moving at a fast clip, springtime breezes lifted her hair and sunshine lightened her mood. She stuck her chin skyward, closing her eyes toward the warmth and laughing at Julie's stories. It was easy to forget her troubles here. She had Simone to thank for persuading her to make this trip early. "Simone." She smacked her wrist to her forehead. "Sorry, Julie. Have to text my friend."

"No problem. Say hello to her for me, will you?"

Her thumbs worked fast, and she sent the message that all was well, she'd landed safely. And after she was through with her message and tucked her phone back into her purse, Julie pulled the car into the driveway. "Here we are."

"Wow," Taylor said, taking in the house she hadn't seen since Aunt Suzie died some seven years ago. "It looks great. But it's blue, not yellow anymore."

"Miguel helped me pick out the cornflower blue." Julie parked the car. "The yellow was faded and we wanted to replace it with something more vibrant."

"It's pretty, especially against the white trim and shutters." The property was several acres of rolling meadow that once had been farmland. For three young children spending the summer together, it had been the perfect place to explore. There was a tree house back behind the barn that Julie's dad had built. Was it still there? And what about the gazebo where they'd played endless games? "I really like it."

"Thanks, we thought we needed a change since Dad's giving us the house as a wedding present."

"That's so sweet of Uncle Zach."

"Yeah, he's a doll. He moved into a senior living apartment a month ago. I miss him. But he insisted a married couple needed their privacy and claimed he couldn't keep up with the house anymore. Personally, I think it's hard for him living here without Mom. I think he's enjoying his new place."

"Change can be good, I suppose," she said without much enthusiasm.

The changes she'd gone through lately hadn't been remotely good. But she was going to have to adjust her attitude. She didn't want to bring Julie down.

"Thinking about your situation?"

"Mmm, trying not to, but every so often, my stomach dips at all the unknowns in my life now. But I *promise* not to dwell. I wouldn't do that to you. Besides, I'm stoked about being your maid of honor."

"I wouldn't have anyone but you. Come on, I want to introduce you to Muffy."

"Muffy? I can't wait."

"Just hold on to your hat, she's still a pup and she's got a lot of energy."

Julie helped with her luggage and together they entered the house. Immediately, a blond and white ball of fluff barreled toward them, lifting off on all fours to greet Julie. Once, twice, three times, until her tongue lagged out of her sweet little fur face and big, round, deep chocolate eyes implored Julie for attention.

Julie dropped the luggage and bent down. "Okay, Muffy. I'm here. Don't you worry now." Julie's soft tone calmed the pup as she absorbed the love. If she was a cat, she'd be purring.

"She's darling."

Julie snuggled her. "And a handful and a half."

Taylor bent to her knees too and rubbed her behind the ears. "Hi, Muffy. I'm Taylor."

Muffy craned her neck over, darted her tongue out and slurped a wet kiss to her chin.

Taylor chuckled. "You're fast."

"You don't know the half of it. If the door is open, she takes it as a personal invitation and out she goes racing down the street. I've had to chase her down three times this week. She's signed up for obedience school after our honeymoon, because she's a naughty little girl." Julie said the last part with the teeniest, tiny loving voice.

"Does she know her way home yet?"

"I wish. But, unfortunately, she has no feline tendencies."

"Meaning, she gets lost?"

"When she takes off, she's too excited to know where the heck she is. Luckily, I've always been able to find her."

Muffy sounded like a lot of trouble. But she was adorable, so that made up for some of it.

"Well," Julie said, picking up the terrier mix and standing, "you must be tired. Do you want to settle in and rest?" Julie glanced at the staircase just off the living room. "Your room's all ready for you. We haven't changed a thing."

Muffy gave Julie another wet kiss.

"Ah, I love that room." It was a bedroom that overlooked the backyard and the hills behind. Taylor would stare out that window often, waking at the crack of dawn and waiting for the rest of the family to rise. Back then, they had goats and chickens. "I'm actually good. Just let me unpack and I'll meet you down here and we'll talk some more."

"Oh, I was hoping you'd say that. I'm dying to see my gown. Do you think I could?"

"Well, I don't usually show my work until it's all finished."

Hope died in Julie's eyes until Taylor grinned. "Kidding. Of course you can see your gown. You can try it on."

"Oh no. Not me. I'm a hot mess right now. I've been running around all day and still smell of crayons, glue and finger paint."

Julie was a grade school teacher. She did look a bit frazzled at the moment, but in a good way. "Would you mind putting it on for me?" Julie scrunched up her nose. "Just for a sec?"

"You are not a hot mess. But if it'll make you happy, I'll model the dress for you. Just remember it's not finished. There's a whole lot more detailing that needs to be added."

"I know. I'm just excited to see it in person."

"I'll go up now. Be back down in ten."

"Sounds perfect. I'll help you bring up your bags."

"No need. I've got it. Just get ready for my grand entrance."

Julie nuzzled Muffy's head. "Did you hear that? I'm getting my very own fashion show," she told the pup.

And minutes later, Taylor was unpacked and dressed in Julie's off-one-shoulder Cinderella dress. She had to admit the gown traveled well. So, no worries there. And the veil was a perfect match.

"Ready or not, here I come," she called out.

"All ready down here," Julie practically squealed from the base of the stairs.

Taylor began her descent gracefully, the French taffeta fabric parting with ease as she took each step, the train behind her fanning out in grand Scarlett O'Hara fashion.

Tears entered Julie's eyes and there was no mistaking the emotion on her face. This was why Taylor loved designing gowns. This was the big payoff, seeing the joy on the bride-to-be's face. She didn't always get that honor or had the luxury but today, because it was Julie, Taylor was able to witness it firsthand.

"It's...breathtaking, Taye."

Taylor made it down the staircase, just as Julie's cell phone rang. Julie frowned and broke eye contact to glance at the phone on the entry table, clearly unhappy this special moment had been interrupted. "It's Miguel. I'd better get this."

Taylor nodded.

"Hi. What's up... Oh no. Miguel, I'll be right there. No, don't call a tow service. I'm coming to get you."

"What's wrong?" Taylor asked as Julie put down the phone.

"Miguel's car died right in the middle of town. Do you mind if I go get him? I shouldn't be long."

"You don't have to ask. Go, get your fiancé. I'll be here when you get home, not to worry."

"Okay, thanks! I won't be long."

"Take as much time as you need..."

Julie was already heading for the front door before all the words were out.

Julie started up her car in the driveway and took off down the street.

Just as she was ready to head back upstairs, she noticed Julie left the front door ajar.

And then she caught sight of Muffy's wiggling little blond bottom scooting out the door.

"No, Muffy! No. Come back! Muffy, Muffy!"

The little tyrant didn't hesitate, not even for a second. By the time Taylor made it to the door, the pup was zipping down the street.

Taylor had no choice. She didn't have a second to spare as Julie's words echoed in her ears.

When she takes off, she's too excited to know where the heck she is.

Taylor couldn't lose Muffy or, heaven forbid, have something happen to her. She lifted the hem of her dress, and flew down the steps, racing as fast as her legs and French taffeta would let her. Luckily, the dog was in sight, but she didn't know for how long, Muffy was lengthening her lead.

"Stop, Muffy! Stop!"

The dog raced in the opposite direction of town, to where the street became a country road. Taylor's heart pounded, her breath came in short, quick spurts. She was losing ground. The dog was getting away. She picked up her pace, fighting dirt clods and hopping over potholes in the road.

Just then, a shiny red pickup truck came up behind her. She untangled the veil from her face as the truck slowed and she glanced into the cab, hoping for a miracle.

And found a handsome Stetson-wearing man checking her out from the very top of her lace veil to the hand-stitched hem of her skirt and everywhere in between. He did a double-take, then his lips lifted in a definite smirk.

If she wasn't entirely certain who the blue-eyed guy was, the logo on the side door gave it away.

Cooper Construction.

Shoot.

Her heart did a little flip and her throat locked up good and tight. Ryan "Coop" Cooper was so *not* her miracle. Yet he looked better than her crazy daydreams.

"Hey, Taylor," he drawled slow and easy-like. "What poor guy are you running away from this time?"

Chapter Three

COOP COULDN'T BELIEVE his eyes. He stared out the window of his truck. The girl in the runaway bride getup was Taylor Preston. And she was prettier than he recalled. All that silky dark hair, those wide green-as-grass eyes kind of punched him in the gut. Sure, he'd known she was due back in town for the wedding. He'd heard enough about it from Miguel and Julie, but seeing her again, in the flesh, wearing that damn wedding outfit, just about knocked his boots off. It shouldn't. It'd been almost twelve years, but first loves died hard, and she had been all that.

"Funny, Coop. Real…funny," she said, her labored breaths bringing her chest up and down. She was definitely winded. "I'm after Julie's dog, she escaped."

"Need some help?"

She glanced at him, frowning. His earlier comment didn't set well with her, he figured. But he couldn't just leave her to chase the dog by herself.

She squinted down the road and finally nodded. "Yes."

"I'll find her," he said, realizing now wasn't the time to reminisce. "Wait here. Catch your breath." He tossed her a bottle of water and was surprised that she'd caught it. He didn't miss the grudging acceptance in her eyes. "Drink. I'll be back in a minute."

"She...could...be anywhere," she said, heaving another breath, her cheeks flushed with color.

"I'll find her," he said a second time, gunning the engine and pulling away, catching a glimpse of her reflection in the rearview mirror. She was standing there, looking a little dumbfounded and beautiful as ever in that fancy wedding gown.

Coop sighed. She was another lifetime ago. And this was now.

He scanned the landscape, looking for the pup, and when he thought he spotted her, a little speck of blond against the green shrubs, he stopped the truck and got out. He put two fingers in his mouth and whistled once, twice, and then called the dog by name. "Here, Muffin."

The pup lifted her head up from the brush, spotted him, thought about it a second, then put her tail between her legs and curled her body in a defensive posture as she ambled over.

"Muffin, where do you think you're going, girl?"

Her tail began to wag. She recognized his voice.

Coop bent and gave the dog a pat behind her ears. "Don't you know it's a dangerous world out there? Sometimes, when you go running off, you can't find your way back home."

The irony was killing him. Here he was giving the pup a sermon about leaving behind those who love you, when the epitome of that very thing was marching up the road, clutching handfuls of white fabric, her long dark hair catching the breeze. He picked up the dog and walked back to his truck. By that time, Taylor made her way over.

"Thank goodness you found her," she said, her voice tight, the relief on her face almost tangible. "I'd never forgive myself if something happened to her."

"No harm, no foul," Coop said, rising with the pup in his arms. He couldn't say the same about the two of them. There'd been plenty of harm. "You through with your water?"

Taylor glanced at her right hand, looking a bit shocked that she still held the bottle. "Uh, yeah."

Coop reached for it, his fingers brushing over her delicate hand. The moment froze in time, and they gazed deep into each other's eyes. Her lips were pink, her cheeks flushed and her green eyes were just as large and expressive as he'd remembered. They'd been friends, then more than friends, and all of that was reflected in her eyes, on her expression.

He cleared his throat and directed his attention to the dog. "Here you go, Muffin." He poured water into her mouth and the parched pup lapped it up.

"I thought her name was Muffy."

Coop smiled slow and steady now. "She's Muffy to everyone but me."

"Oh, I see. And why is that?"

"Because Muffin's her real name."

"Says Coop, the guy who's gone by his shortened last name for his entire life."

"Says the girl who was chasing down a dog in someone else's weddin' gown."

She gave him her chin. "How do you know it's not my…my wedding gown."

Hell if it was. His brows lifted. "Is it?"

She shook her head. "No. Do people still call you Co-op?"

He eyed her. "Most people do. My wife used to call me Ryan." Coop took a swallow, wondering why on earth he just told her that.

He didn't talk about Francine. Not to anyone. She'd been gone for three years and still the pain gnawed in his gut.

"Get in. I'll give you a ride back to Julie's."

Taylor was silent as she opened the door and climbed into the cab of the truck.

He tucked Muffin over the Silverado's side panel and set her inside the bed. "Lie down," he said firmly. The dog did as she was told and set her head on her front paws. She gazed up at him, looking remorseful. "Stay."

"Is she safe back there?" Taylor asked.

"Should be. Didn't want her dirty paws ruining the gown."

"It'll be an easy fix," she said, unconcerned.

She was a big fashion designer now. She'd gone after her dream and had achieved it. At least losing her had meant something. At least she'd been the success she'd always wanted to be, so it wasn't all for nothing.

"I'm sorry about your wife, Coop," she said quietly. "I didn't hear about it right away. I'm…it must have been hard."

Her voice held too much sympathy, too much understanding. He didn't know what to do with that. He couldn't say, "It's okay." Because it wasn't. He couldn't pass off Francine's death as something frivolous. Losing her had been monumental and put a giant hole in his heart. "We met when I was living in LA."

She nodded and turned her body toward him. "You have a child?"

Coop couldn't keep the smile off his face. His daughter was a bright spot in his life. "Cassie, yeah. She's eight. We live with my father now. Dad was getting up in age and Cassie needed the stability so we moved back here."

"You're working construction with your dad?"

"Dad's mostly retired. He's Grandpa Joe now, and helps out with Cassie."

"I bet he loves that. Your dad was always good with kids."

"Yeah, he does." Coop gave her a glance, their eyes connecting.

He had to stop looking at her like she was the girl he

knew, the girl he'd played with every summer. The girl who'd stolen his young heart. He didn't know Taylor at all anymore. She had a whole life back in New York. And he'd moved on too, their lives taking completely different paths. He couldn't forget Francine and how much she'd meant him. How she'd filled a void in his life and gave him a daughter. Seeing Taylor again after all this time shouldn't matter. It didn't. She was once his friend and that was how he'd leave it, despite the green eyes and familiar pretty face. Despite her long, dark wavy hair and contagious smile.

He started the engine and made a U-turn with his truck, keeping his gaze focused on the road. Taylor was quiet on the short drive and he wasn't about to encourage any more conversation. Once he pulled up to Julie's house, he set the parking brake and gave her a glance.

Her eyes fluttered and she sighed, as if the weight of the world rested on her shoulders. What was with her, running around in that getup, showing up three weeks early to Last Stand? Yeah, he'd noticed.

"Well, thanks for the ride," she said, breaking the awkward silence. "And for the rescue." It struck him how she sat in the passenger seat with all that ivory cascading around her like a porcelain doll encased in folds of material. "I don't think I would've caught up to Muffy without your help."

"No problem." He got out of the truck.

Taylor climbed out too, struggling with the gown a bit as she met him around the back end, where Muffy was waiting, her paws scratching at the tailgate.

"I'll get her," Taylor said. "No need to delay you any longer. Thanks again." She reached in just as the dog leapt into her arms.

Traitor.

Taylor held the puppy firmly under her arm and began walking toward the house. He was two steps behind her and when she turned, her brows gathered in puzzlement. "We're fine now, Coop. You don't have to—"

"I was heading to Julie's when I spotted you."

"Oh, uh. To see me?"

He supposed it was only natural for her to think that. "I have an appointment with Miguel."

Pink color touched her cheeks again. He recalled her getting flustered a lot when they were younger. He used to think she was a sissy, until that last year, when he found her blushing totally adorable. It still was pretty darn cute.

"Miguel isn't here right now. He had some car trouble and Julie went to pick him up."

"That's okay. I'll wait," he said and when she stepped into the house, he followed her inside.

She put the dog down and made sure the front door was sufficiently shut and locked behind him.

She smiled. "Don't want another escape on my watch."

"That's probably wise."

"So, uh, would you like to sit down?" she asked.

"I will in a second. So, is that Julie's gown you're wearing?" There were smudges on the front of the dress, along with a hem that had picked up a lot of Texas red dirt.

"Yes."

"Your design?"

"My design. I was trying it on for her when she got the call from Miguel. She took off quickly."

"And left the door open?"

She nodded and shot daggers at the dog lying lazily by the fireplace now. "That little booger sure can run fast."

He chuckled, finding the lopsided veil on her head, the crumpled mess of a gown and her particular expression right now pretty darn comical. As least some things about Taylor hadn't changed. She could still make him laugh. "She did give you a run for your money. Good thing I came along when I did."

"Yeah...good thing." Though when he'd driven up, she'd looked anything but happy to see him.

Their eyes met and he couldn't quite look away. "Are you sure you can clean the dress?"

"I'm sure. It'll look like new when I'm through with it."

"You're talented, Taylor," he said, removing his smile. He meant it.

"I, uh...apparently I'm not talented enough. I got fired," she blurted. Eyes wide, her hand went to her mouth and the rosy color came back to her cheeks. "I can't believe I just told you that."

Voices coming from the front door put them on alert.

"Oh no. They're back. Miguel can't see this dress," she told him as she scrambled behind him. "Hide me."

"Hide you?" What on earth?

Taylor's arms came around his torso, and she pressed the side of her head to his back. She was using him as a visual blockade. "Isn't it that the groom can't see the *bride* in her wedding gown?"

"I'm not taking any chances with Julie's happiness," she whispered.

"Miguel," she called out. He was almost fully inside the house now. "Close your eyes! Please."

Julie explained the situation to him and then Miguel answered, "Oooo-kay. Eyes are shut."

"Walk me to the stairs, Coop. Just in case."

This was insane, but Coop wasn't about to argue with a centuries-old tradition. Even if Taylor wasn't the bride. They sort of penguin-walked toward the stairs, Taylor tucked safely behind his back, and once she reached the base of the stairs, she made a quick dash. "All clear," she called down once she was upstairs and out of sight.

Coop stood there, facing an amused Julie and Miguel.

He shook his head, ignoring the twinkle in their eyes.

And realized nothing much was *all clear* when it came to Taylor Preston.

"MIGUEL MUST THINK I'm a total idiot," Taylor said to Julie.

She sat at the kitchen table, wearing a pair of white capris and a denim shirt knotted at the waist, sipping iced tea and glancing out the big window in the kitchen. The men were in the backyard beyond the pool area, in deep discussion. Coop's appointment with Miguel.

"Not at all, Taye. He's grateful you're here. It takes the pressure off him to help me with the wedding plans. Now I have you." She grinned. "And just for the record, he thinks you're amazing for caring so much about tradition."

"Really?"

"I wouldn't lie to you."

"Well, then. I only feel stupid in front of Coop now."

"He doesn't think you're stupid."

She lifted the glass to her lips. "I wouldn't count on that. Why is he here anyway?"

"Miguel's giving me a she-shed as a wedding present, right there where the old gazebo stands. The gazebo going's down and the she-shed is going up."

"Wow, you're getting your own she-shed. That's an amazing gift. You've always wanted a little library, reading area all your own."

"Yep." Julie shrugged. "You know me, always with my nose in a book."

"There's nothing wrong with that. But I'm sorry to see the gazebo go."

Julie shot her a knowing look. "Me too. We had fun times playing in it. But it's old and falling apart now, and that space is perfect for the shed. Not too far away from the house, and close enough to the twin cottonwoods to supply some shade. Miguel has one vice, if you can call it that, he likes music. Loud music. And he figured once we marry and he moves in, it'll save us arguments." She rolled her eyes. "He's pretty addicted to heavy metal."

"Ugh, say no more."

They looked at each other and laughed. Both of them loved soft country rock. It was as adventurous as they would ever get, musically speaking.

"My admiration for your fiancé just bumped up a notch."

Julie peered out the window, and seeing Miguel, a soft glow stole over her face. "Yeah, he's pretty amazing."

"You two wrote the book on love," Taylor said. "You're a good match."

"Except for his taste in music. So, what about you? Have you been dating anyone?"

"Me? No. I haven't had a date in at least a year. I've been too busy for all the complications of a relationship."

Julie put a plate of chocolate chip cookies on the table. It reminded Taylor of old times, when Aunt Suzie would serve them sweets. Julie set two napkins out. "You know, relationships don't have to be complicated. The best ones are sort of simple. I mean, you find the right one and suddenly things fall into place."

"In a perfect world."

"No, in a world where you have your priorities straight."

Taylor bit down on a cookie and all sorts of good things happened in her mouth. "These are fantastic. Your mom's recipe?"

"Of course. Hey, I saw how you changed the subject. Did you think I wouldn't notice?"

"Okay, guilty as charged, but the cookies really are delicious."

"Thanks. So, what did you think of Coop?" Julie asked matter-of-factly.

"Coop? I've only spent a few minutes with him. Chasing Muffy." She rolled her eyes. "And using him as a human shield. Made quite an impression, I'm sure."

"You two were best friends once upon a time. Yet, you rarely asked about him or wanted to know what was happening in his life. And, remember, it's me you're talking to."

Meaning, no bluffing. "I didn't ask about him, because…well, there was no reason to dredge up the past. We'd fallen in love on my last summer here and it was absolutely dreamy. First loves and all that. But the hard truth is I left him for my career and I know I hurt him."

"You were just kids, Taye. Hardly grown up enough to know what you were feeling."

"Are you saying I didn't break his heart?"

"Uh, well…" Julie's voice surged up an octave. "That did

happen."

"See? I spent quite a few years feeling horrible about that. And after coming back here, he's the first person I run into."

"Must be fate," Julie teased.

"Must be small towns. Hardly a day goes by when you don't run into somebody you know. It was what made Last Stand so different than New York. Everyone seems to know each other. Everyone is friendly. Not so much in my town."

"Personally, I'm glad Coop's back," Julie said. "He and Miguel hit it off right away when Coop returned last year. He's a really good friend and..."

"And?"

"And quite a hunk."

"I haven't noticed." Those big strong arms, wide shoulders and blue river eyes.

Julie bit into another cookie. "Okay, have it your way. But just think how cool it would be if you two—"

"Uh-uh. Don't even go there. I'm here for your wedding and to figure out my next career move...that's if I even have a career anymore."

Miguel and Coop walked into the kitchen. "Wow, smells like your mom's famous chocolate chip cookies in here," Coop said. "Am I right?"

Julie pointed to the empty seats at the table. "Sit down and find out for yourself. I'll get you some iced tea."

"I won't say no," Coop said, taking a seat. "Mind if I take one home for Cassie?"

"Sure. I'll pack you a goodie bag before you leave," Julie said. "Give some to your dad too."

"Thanks."

"So," Miguel began, taking the last seat at the table. "Looks like Coop is ready to break ground in two days."

"Two days? That's great news," Julie said, pouring two glasses of iced tea. "I'm pretty jazzed about it."

"Yeah, first thing we'll do is get the demolition crew to take down the gazebo."

Taylor locked gazes with him and, for a brief moment, she knew what he was thinking, what she was witnessing in his eyes. Over the years, the gazebo had become something special to them—the promises they'd made to one another, the place they'd first kissed. The place they said their heart-wrenching final goodbye. All of that flashed between them, a lightning rod of memories striking with quick precision. And then, it was gone, as quickly as it had come as both looked away.

"Coop will have it up before the wedding, honey," Miguel said.

"I hope to. If the weather holds. We should have it done in a couple of weeks."

"Really?" Julie asked.

He shrugged. "Can't see why not. We've got all the plans approved and permits are in order."

Julie turned her way. "Miguel has been working with Coop behind my back, making sure it was doable before he told me about it."

"Yeah, this guy's making the rest of us mere mortal men look bad," Coop said.

"I can see that," Taylor said. "Julie loves to be surprised."

"I do. I really do. Don't all women?"

Miguel looked at her. "Do you like surprises, Taylor?"

"Only the happy ones. I mean I was surprised today when Muffy ran away. That wasn't such a good surprise. I didn't know what to do but run after her. Gosh, I still feel badly about that."

"It all ended well," Julie said graciously.

"Because Coop came to the rescue," she added.

Gosh, she could've ruined Julie's gown if he hadn't come along when he had. The only saving grace was that she would've worked night and day to sew a whole new one. Luckily, it hadn't come to that.

Seeing Coop was a big surprise too. Even though Taylor knew he'd moved back to town, she hadn't expected to see him while wearing Julie's wedding gown during the Great Muffy Chase.

Coop stuffed another cookie in his mouth and then pushed back his chair. "Well, I'd best get going." He glanced at his watch. "Cassie's got a ball game in an hour. And a coach has to do what a coach has to do."

"Does Cassie play soccer?" Taylor asked. She'd never played sports during the school year, but during the summers, they'd kick around a soccer ball.

"Nope, she plays first base," Coop said, unable to hide his pride.

"Softball?"

"She's on a boy's baseball team."

"She's one of the best players on the Tigers," Miguel added. "That little girl can hit."

Coop smiled. "She gets it from her father."

"And her coach," Julie added with a wink.

"I'd best be going. Coach can't be late to the game."

And with that Cooper left the kitchen.

"Oh, shoot," Julie said, "I forgot to give him the cookies. Taylor, would you mind?" she said, setting a bunch of cookies onto a paper plate and covering it with plastic wrap. "Go give this to him, before he takes off." Julie shoved the plate in her hands.

She had no time to refuse. Miguel was right there, he could've done it, but Julie's agenda was glaring and brightly written all over her face.

"Sure, I'll just chase him down the way I did Muffy," she said, plate in hand.

She ran out the front door and caught him just as he was getting into his truck. "Wait up, Coop."

He spotted her and leaned against the door, his hat plopped on his head, arms folded, casual as you please and waited for her to reach him. "Are you chasing *me* this time? Never thought I'd see the day."

She looked him up and down, liking him in blue plaid

and jeans a little too much. He'd grown into a beautiful man. His comment, though, rubbed her the wrong way. *And you never will.* She bit her tongue because he was widower now and not the same Coop she could tease endlessly. "You forgot the cookies." She handed him the plate and that was supposed to be that, until she added, "And just for the record, I'm not accustomed to chasing either men or dogs."

Shoot, had she really said that?

He grinned. "Good to know. Thank Julie for the cookies," he said, climbing into the truck. "See you around, Taylor. And that's a promise."

Their eyes met and held for a moment and then he gunned the engine and drove off.

Over the years they'd played the promise game, hiding their promises in the little box Coop had built Taylor after that first summer. It was supposed to be her treasure box, but it served a better purpose housing their end-of-summer promises. *Treasures* of a different kind.

It was old news now, a silly pastime from their childhood.

But promises still meant something to Taylor. And she had no doubt they meant something to Coop too. She also had no doubt she would be seeing a lot of Coop while she was back in Last Stand. There was absolutely no escaping it.

COOP WALKED INTO the barn, otherwise known as Cooper Construction's workshop and found his dad using an electric chop saw to miter the edges of the new baseboard he was installing in the parlor. Now that Grandpa Joe was retired, the guy found more than enough projects to do around the house while Cassie was in school. Sometimes, his dad would work alongside him too.

Coop never once regretted giving up his life in Los Angeles, managing the business end of a flourishing building company, to move back home. Last Stand meant a slower pace of living, more time with his daughter and, most importantly, it meant being with family. Namely his dad. Cassie needed the stability and she loved riding horses, playing baseball, helping him out on weekends. It didn't make up for losing her mother, but it had eased the pain somewhat. For him too.

His dad shut down the saw and looked his way. "Thought you were coaching the game today?"

"I am. I'm running a bit late, is all."

"That have anything to do with Taylor Preston coming back to town?"

Coop stared at his pop. "What? How'd you hear so quickly?" Sometimes, he swore his father was clairvoyant or something. And sometimes, small towns were just too damn small.

"You just told me." His dad grinned and focused on the next plank of baseboard he was readying to cut. "Didn't figure it'd take you very long to reconnect with Taylor."

"We didn't reconnect. Heck, I found her on the road chasing down Muffin and helped get her back to Julie's house."

"That explains the puppy dog look on your face." His dad chuckled thinking himself very funny. He aligned the wood at a forty-five-degree angle and turned on the saw again, making the next cut.

Thoughts of Taylor in that wedding gown filled Coop's head again. She looked beautiful in that thing, and exasperated too. Chasing a pup in a wedding gown? Who would've thunk it? Certainly not him. When he first spotted a bride taking off like there was no tomorrow, he'd thought it curious, wondering what she'd been running from, or who. When he'd come eye to eye with the girl underneath all that snowy white material and discovered it was Taylor, old feelings returned, sort of biting him in the butt. A sense of déjà vu had set in. He'd daydreamed about marrying her so many times in his young life, that it had all seemed surreal when he'd come face-to-face to her in that gown.

"Pop, ancient history, remember?"

"You know what they say, history has a way of repeating itself."

His dad meant well. He didn't want Coop to be alone the rest of his life, but he'd honestly made peace with it. He had Cassie, his dad and a good business that afforded him time to coach his daughter and be home for dinner every night. After Francine died, he didn't think he'd know a truly happy day, but he'd come through on the other side, because he had to. For Cassie. But that didn't mean it hadn't been difficult, it hadn't destroyed him inside. Hadn't made him ward off relationships.

So his dad, and Julie for that matter, were way off base.

He wasn't going to get involved with any woman right now, especially one who'd already broken his heart once.

"Daddy, I'm ready."

Cassie entered the barn in her orange-striped Tigers uniform. Wearing her usual blond braids under a ball cap, and a big smile, she was the brightest spot in his world. "Hey, Cass. You ready to give those Cardinals a day to remember?"

Cassie locked her hands, put out her arms and took an air swing with an invisible bat. "They don't stand a chance," she said.

"I like that spirit, Cass," Grandpa Joe said. "But remember, don't get overconfident. Sometimes, the other team might just surprise you."

"That's what Coach says too," Cassie replied.

"Yeah, well, that's because we're related."

Cassie giggled.

"But it's true," Grandpa Joe said. "Just play your best game, that's all anyone can ask."

"Coach says that too."

Coop put his hand on Cassie's shoulder and gave a squeeze. She was the best part of him and Francine and he was reminded of it every day. "I think it's time to get to the field."

"Yep, it's time to destroy." She turned to her grandfather. "You're coming to the game, aren't you, Grandpa?"

"When have I ever missed one of your games? I'll be along in a little while. See you at the field," he said, giving Cassie a kiss on the forehead.

"Love you, Grandpa," she said, grabbing him around the waist and giving him a hug.

"I love you too, kiddo." His eyes misted up. He was such a sucker for Cassie, but then, who wasn't?

"Let's get going." Coop took Cassie's hand, wondering how many more years she would allow him to do it. He sighed inside; his child was growing up way too fast.

TAYLOR HADN'T SLEPT so well in ages, and as she rose from bed this morning, her body and soul thanked her for the distinct change of scenery. From high-rise buildings to rolling hillsides. It sure made quite a difference in her demeanor. She yawned and stretched her arms over her head as she gazed out the window. The sun was just rising, casting a golden tint to the knolls beyond. Julie's backyard was in full bloom right now with red and yellow roses, daylilies and an assortment of flowery scrubs. Further beyond, hearty bluebonnets blanketed the meadows where they used to play.

A rooster cock-a-doodle-doo-ed and blue jays fluttered through tree branches.

Texas in the spring.

She dressed in her workout clothes, black pants and a teal blue stretchy top, and put her hair up in a ponytail. Back home, she usually worked out in a gym, but the day was far too glorious for staying inside. Once she tied her shoes, she descended the stairs quietly and made sure Muffy was nowhere in sight before she opened the front door and stepped outside, shutting the door firmly behind her.

She walked at a fast pace until her muscles warmed up and then began a slow and easy jog down the road. She was not a pro at running, far from it, her pace just comfortable enough for head clearing. Simone had been right, she'd needed to get away and now as the fog in her brain lifted, she was beginning to see an inkling of light filtering through. It was progress.

Ten minutes into the run, she rounded the corner on Main heading away from town, her eyes trained on the ground as all sorts of freeing thoughts filled her head. The roar of squealing brakes abruptly stopped her in her tracks, her heels digging into the broken road. As she looked up, she faced down the front end of a truck, the engine's heat billowing out. The Silverado came to a careening stop, two feet from her toes. She began to tremble. Her heart pounded harder than it ever had before.

Coop climbed out of his truck and ran over to her. "Taylor, are you okay?"

Dumbfounded, she stared at him. "I think so." She blinked several times.

"Thank goodness." He seemed truly relieved he hadn't flattened her like an iron on wrinkles. But he wasn't half as glad about it as she was.

Once she got her wits about her, she met his eyes. "You almost hit me."

"Dang it, I could have. Good thing I spotted you as I turned the corner. What were you doing running in the middle of the street like that?" His concerned expression turned to anger. "That was a fool thing to do."

"You almost mow me down on the street and it's my fault?"

"That's just it, Taye, you came out of nowhere. It's a good thing I saw you. You should be thanking me."

She gave him the point of her chin. No way was she going to thank him. "You were going too fast."

"I was going below the speed limit." His blue eyes roamed over her, checking her out from top to bottom as if making sure she wasn't going to die of fright or anything. "C'mon, I'll take you back to Julie's." He headed back to his truck.

She wanted to stay put, to tell him her run wasn't over yet and he didn't need to rescue her again, but darn it. She was stupidly scared. Another half a second and she would have been roadkill. So, she buttoned her lip and slow walked back to his truck, making him wait.

Which he did because, basically, he was good guy. She climbed into his truck for the second time in two days, and sat quietly as he gave her a look, sighed deeply then started the engine again.

They were back at Julie's in less than three minutes. He parked the truck and turned to her. "You gonna tell me why you were running down the middle of the street?"

"You gonna call me a fool again?"

"No."

"You gonna think it?"

He half smiled and his grim face lightened up. "Maybe."

"You!" She wanted to swat at him, give him a punch in the arm or something like she used to, but she wasn't a kid anymore. So, she held back and then the words started spilling out, because this was Coop and he'd always been a good listener. "I wasn't thinking about traffic at this hour. I was feeling unburdened and the road under my feet felt freeing. It's not as if I can run like this in New York. It's all so different. My frustrations lessened with every step and I guess I got lost in all that, until I faced down your big red hulk of a truck."

"At least you weren't wearing a wedding dress this time." He didn't need to point out the obvious and rub it in. "Good thing I had a double espresso this morning. Kept me on my toes."

"And off mine."

He grinned. "What are you doing today?"

"I'll be working on Julie's gown. And once she's home from school, we're going cake tasting. Nothing that can get me flattened."

"Then I approve."

"Good. I was worried. Wouldn't want you coming to my rescue a third time."

"Just promise me if you continue jogging, you'll be more careful. Not everyone has quick reactions."

She titled her head and regarded him, taking him seriously now. He wasn't being glib. He seemed truly concerned and that put a smile around her heart. "I promise."

"I LOVE IT." Julie gazed at her reflection in the mirror, a big smile on her face. She'd had parent-teacher conferences today, which meant no glue or crayons or paint, so as soon as she arrived home, she asked to try on her dress. "It's absolutely perfect. Just what I wanted, Taylor. You promised me a gorgeous gown and you delivered."

"I'm glad you like it, hon." And she was doubly glad she was able to give the dress a good cleaning. The stains were only on the surface and they'd come out without a problem.

Julie moved from side to side, twirled around in her mother's master bedroom, which was now her own, never once taking her eyes off the gown.

The sign of a satisfied bride.

"Mom would've loved it." Then Julie's face fell, the hurt behind her eyes clearly evident.

Taylor understood that look, the pain and loss that Julie was feeling as she touched the side of the veil, fingering the fine lace.

Taylor came up beside her and squeezed her shoulders, looking at her through her reflection in the mirror. "She's here with you, Jules. Always. As long as you keep her memory close to your heart."

"You think so?"

"I know so."

"Here I am going on, when you lost your mother too. Auntie Sable was a great woman."

"She was. And I miss her every day. But you know what?" She perked up her voice deliberately to change the mood. "This is a fun day and we're going to keep it that way. Now where are Aunt Suzie's pearls you wanted to wear with the dress?"

"I have them right here." Julie rummaged through a five-tiered jewelry box, coming up with a crushed velvet necklace box. She opened it and weaved her hands through the pearls. "Aren't they beautiful?"

"They are."

Julie roped the long strand around her neck and faced the mirror. "Oh, no. Gosh," she said quietly, frowning at her reflection, tears touching her eyes. "What do you think?"

The pearls were clearly not a match to the dress and Julie's expression said it all. She'd had her heart set on wearing them. It was important for her to feel close to her mother on her wedding day. It was always in the plan.

But now, seeing the pearls lying over the bodice of the gown, Taylor hated to admit they were an eyesore. "I think...we'll work around it."

Julie's shoulders slumped, her mouth turned downward. "How?"

Taylor shifted her mind into design mode. The gown she'd fashioned for Julie was an off-one-shoulder angular design that was held together by a thin strap overlaid with lace from front to back. Perhaps a choker or a shorter strand of pearls might've worked around her neck but this long strand clearly didn't. Unless...

"Julie, take off the pearls. I have an idea."

And once she had the pearls in hand, she doubled them up and set them over Julie's shoulder. "What if we use them as your strap? They're delicate enough not to look obtrusive. I can sew them on from front to back with a bit of lace underneath and then add some pearl details to the bodice, to make it all look cohesive? See, it would go from here to here." Taylor demonstrated her idea. "I promise you, I won't damage the pearls in any way, and it'll look as if it was the original plan."

"I was going to wear a pair of pearl and diamond earrings." There was hope in Julie's voice.

"That's perfect," Taylor said. "With the decorative pearl strap and earrings, you won't need a necklace at all. The only thing prettier than the gown itself will be the bride wearing it."

"That's sweet, coz." Julie's expression softened. "And I love the idea. Mom will be with me, just like I wanted. You sure solved the problem in a quick hurry. Must mean only one thing. You're a genius, Taylor."

"I'm not, but go on, keep talking." She motioned with her hand to keep the compliments coming.

Julie giggled and wrapped her up in a big warm hug. "You are the best, Taylor. Thanks."

"Don't thank me yet, I still have to hem the dress and make the bustle and then do a final fitting."

"I have no doubt you'll crush it."

Crush it? She almost *was* crushed today, but she wasn't going to bring that up to her cousin. She'd rather forget about what happened during her jog this morning, forget about the panic in Coop's eyes when he'd thought he might've injured her.

"You have so much faith in me," she told Julie.

"I do. If I didn't, I wouldn't have asked you to help pick out my wedding cake."

Taylor smiled. "I have to admit, it sounds like fun, but I'm feeling a little guilty. Shouldn't Miguel be in on this?"

"If he can get away from work, he'll join us. Techy problems never end. I guess that's a good thing or my soon-to-be-husband wouldn't have a job."

"Computers, can't live *with* them, can't live *without* them."

They looked at each other and giggled, Julie taking her hand and squeezing. "I'm so glad you're here, Taye. And it's not just because you made me the most beautiful gown in the world or the help you're giving me. I've missed you. I used to love all those summers we spent together."

"I've missed you too. I have the best memories of Last Stand. Seeing each other once in a while doesn't seem like quite enough, does it?" She smiled at her cousin.

Julie was like a sister to her, and it was never more evident than right now as they worked on the wedding together.

"No, it doesn't. Wish we could fix that," Julie said with a bit of whimsy. "I mean, you really don't have to go back to New York." She raised her brows expectantly.

"Not for a few weeks."

"That's not what I meant."

Julie stared at her and Taylor was immediately put on guard. She loved it here, but Last Stand wasn't her home. She didn't fit in here, not where it counted. She'd grown up in the big city with traffic and skyscrapers and white Christmases. She'd studied in New York. She'd landed her first job in New York. She had an apartment and friends. Her entire adult life had been filled with big city dreams.

"I love you, but there's no future for me here in Last

Stand. As soon as I get back, I'm going to have to do a full-court press to get a job." She shrugged, hearing the discouragement in her own voice.

She wasn't looking forward to going home and trying to find work. She wasn't good with résumés and talking herself up. In a perfect world, her designs would sell themselves. Like that would ever happen.

For now, she just wanted to pretend she was on a month-long vacation. She wanted to focus on Julie's wedding and forget her problems.

"I have no doubt you'll find work, Taylor. You're too talented not to be noticed. But, can't a bride-to-be do some wishful thinking?"

"Not fair, you're using the bride card."

"Is so fair. I only have a few more weeks with that title."

"Yeah, then you'll be a married woman."

"Hard to believe. It's surreal, you know? Remember all those summers we talked about what our weddings would be like?"

"Of course I remember," she said quietly. They were two young girls with lofty dreams, collecting magazine photos of brides and flowers and wedding venues. "And now, your dreams are coming true. You're getting married to a great guy in a beautiful church in grand fashion."

"Oh, I didn't mean to…to—"

"It's okay, Julie. I figure when the time comes, I'll be ready. I'm not now. So, you don't have to feel even a teensy bit guilty that you found your once-in-a-lifetime guy."

"I don't feel guilty. I just want you to have what I have. I know there's someone wonderful out there for you."

"And when I find love, you'll be the first one I tell."

"Promise?"

"I promise, Jules."

Chapter Four

CAKE TASTING WAS definitely all it was cracked up to be. Taylor's tummy was happy as she bit into exotic cake flavors like vanilla with mango filling, rosemary lemon and pineapple guava. All of them tasted light and refreshing and delicious. But Taylor was and always would be a holdout for chocolate.

"I'm loving the vanilla mango. I think it's a possible maybe," Julie said, putting her fork down. "What do you think?"

This was the third cake they'd tasted that was a possible *maybe*. Julie was really struggling with this decision.

Taylor wouldn't disagree with her. "It's really good."

"Just good?"

Taylor glanced at the baker, who was watching her from behind the counter. "Deliciously good," she said with more enthusiasm. Who wanted to hurt the baker's feelings?

"But you're not sure?" Julie blinked, seeming unusually uncertain.

"I don't have to be sure. You do," she encouraged her as gently as she could. "It's your wedding."

The bakery door opened and Miguel walked in just in time to save the day.

Julie's face lit up. "Miguel. I'm so glad you're here."

Before the door closed, Coop walked into the bakery just behind him and Taylor made eye contact with him. She glanced away quickly. She didn't like lighting up inside seeing him again. No, that was for sweethearts like Miguel and Julie.

"Hi, hon." Miguel bent to give Julie a quick kiss. "Hey, Taylor. You girls making any progress?"

"Not much. They're all so good, it's hard to choose."

"That's why I brought reinforcements. I ran into Coop and invited him to come along."

"Hi," Coop said, all swagger and good looks. "Hope it's okay I'm here."

He looked at Julie first, then swiveled his head to give Taylor a quick glance. He wore a pair of jeans and a blue plaid shirt, a cowboy hat on his head, looking casual and healthy and, well, handsome. She supposed it was inevitable to be running into him often since he was a friend of Miguel and Julie's and he lived just half a mile down the street.

"Sure, it's okay. The more the merrier," Julie said. "I do need a bit of help, I'm having trouble deciding. Why don't you guys try some of these?" She pushed the plates toward them.

Miguel and Coop sat down, Coop removing his hat, and both took a minute to taste everything.

Miguel began nodding his head. “I like them all.”

“Yeah, me too,” Coop said. “I wouldn’t refuse a one of them.”

“But no standouts?”

Before they could answer, the baker came over and laid out two more choices. “Here you go,” she said. “Some classic flavors for you to try. This one is white cake with a lemon chiffon center and this one is raspberry chocolate.”

Both looked tantalizing. Taylor immediately dug in and crossed forks with Coop as they went in for the raspberry chocolate. Their eyes met as their utensils clinked.

“You were always a sucker for chocolate,” he said.

“Me? I wasn’t the one who’d mooch everyone’s candy bars when they weren’t looking. I remember one time at the movies when you broke off a big piece of my Hershey bar without even asking. Before I could say a word, you’d gobbled it down and then gave me a big Cheshire cat smile.”

“I didn’t gobble. Boys don’t gobble.” He shrugged, looking a little remorseful, then took a big bite of cake and swallowed it down. “And I did feel a little guilty about that.”

“Ah-ha! Now you’re sorry. Goodness, you had a sweet tooth back then.” Taylor laid into her cake too. She had to be fast. With Coop around, she wouldn’t get a second bite.

“He still does,” Miguel said, forking a piece too. “That’s another reason I invited him.”

“Yeah, I admit it,” he said. “Chocolate is my one vice.”

“You have only one?” she asked, batting her eyes and

smiling.

"The only one I'm admitting to," he chirped back.

"Coop's right," Julie said. "You're just as guilty, Taye." Julie looked at the piece of cake that was now a plate of crumbs. "I guess I have your answers. Chocolate raspberry."

"It's really delicious," Taylor said.

"At last, we agree on something." Coop winked at her, a move that totally caught her off guard because whenever they'd conspire together, that was what he'd do to seal the deal.

As if the wink meant *I'm with you*. And that one wink sent butterflies swarming around in her tummy. It'd given her a glimpse of the boy he once was, and the man he'd become. And she began feeling things she had no right or reason to feel. Not about Coop.

He wasn't an option.

Miguel spoke up. "Honey, I really think you've found the right one. Everyone seems to like it the best."

She sighed. "It's not light and airy, but…deep and hearty."

Miguel grinned at her. "Just like our love." Corny as it was, Julie's perplexed face melted into a sweet smile and just like that, the decision was made.

Oh, if only life was always that easy.

SATURDAY MORNING, TAYLOR and Julie stepped out onto the back patio, coffee cups in hand, watching a crew of four leather-gloved men wearing hard hats and wielding axes break apart the gazebo. The takedown was hard to watch, both of them quietly observing the destruction of not just a weather-worn structure but the removal of yet one more memory in their lives. Taylor wondered if Julie felt the same sense of loss. Every time something was changed or removed, it was like losing a piece of their mothers all over again. Because the gazebo represented so much more than a fun place to play. It represented their youth, when both their moms were alive and vital. It represented friendship and secrets and first loves and, quite frankly, seeing the gazebo go down was like a sharp prick to the heart. She hadn't expected to be this sad, to feel like another fragment of her family was being taken away.

"I didn't think it'd hurt this bad," Julie said.

Taylor turned to her. "I know. I feel it too. But something wonderful will go up in its place, Jules. Something that represents your future with Miguel."

"I know you're right." She sipped her coffee.

Holding on to the past never did anyone any good. "I think your she-shed is going to be the next generation's gazebo. If you know what I mean. It'll be an icon, just like the gazebo was for us."

"Progress, I guess."

"Yeah."

"I can always build a new one." Coop sidled up next to them, wearing a hard hat, jeans and a pair of scuffed up work boots. The T-shirt he wore looked two sizes too small for his muscular arms. He held a clipboard in his hand and gave them both a good-morning smile. He must've come through the side gate. She hadn't seen him until he was standing right next to her. Before she could catch her breath and stop her heart from speeding up, another hard-hatted Cooper appeared. This one, ten times more adorable. Her long blond braids fell past her shoulders, and in jeans, work boots and a T-shirt, she looked like a mini-Cooper. Not the car, the kid.

"Morning, Cassie," Julie said.

"Hi, Julie."

Coop put his hand on his daughter's shoulder. "Cassie, this is Taylor. She's an old friend."

"Hi."

"Cassie has agreed to be the flower girl in our wedding," Julie explained. "We're going dress shopping tomorrow, right Cass?"

Cassie gave a nod. "I guess so." She didn't look too happy about it.

Taylor bent to shake her hand. "Hi, Cassie. It's nice to meet you. Are you helping your dad today?"

She nodded. "I get to fill the wheelbarrow, but only with the small pieces."

"I'm sure your daddy's happy to have your help today."

"He promised me I could come."

"Well, I'm glad you're here."

"Me too."

"I have an idea," she said, looking from Julie to Cassie. "Why don't I make your flower girl dress for you?"

The girl gazed up at her. "You can do that?"

"I can. And I'd love to." Taylor met her cousin's eyes. "I don't know why you didn't mention it to me before."

"Well, because you were busy in New York and I didn't want to put too much pressure on you."

"But now I'm here and I'm happy to do it. If that's okay with Coop?"

The three females looked to him. He put up his hands. If he had any objection, he wouldn't stand a chance. "Okay by me. That's if it's not too much trouble for you, Taylor."

"Not at all. Would you like that, Cassie?"

"Does that mean I don't have to go shopping for a dress?"

"Cass," her father warned.

"Sorry, Daddy, but I don't like to shop. It's boring. I'd rather practice batting with Grandpa Joe."

Taylor laughed. "You know what? When I was your age, I didn't like shopping either. I'd rather play with my friends. Why don't you come see me after your work is done? I'll take a few measurements and Julie and I will do all the shopping for the material for your dress."

"Really?" Cassie smiled wide and began nodding.

On a sigh, Coop narrowed his eyes on her. "Cassie, what

do you say?"

"Thank you?"

Coop cleared his throat and Taylor stifled another laugh.

"Yes, thank you, Taylor, Julie. We'll see you later in the day. C'mon, Cass, let's get to work."

Cassie saluted. "Aye, aye, captain."

The two walked toward the gazebo, where the crew was hacking away at it.

"She's pretty cute," Taylor said.

"Yeah, she's the apple of Coop's eye. And her Grandpa Joe's too. It's a good thing that Coop came back. He's happier here."

"I can't imagine what it was like for him."

"Yeah, Coop's quiet about it, but I know it ripped him up inside."

Taylor pursed her lips. "I guess he's been hurt enough for two lifetimes. First, I abandoned him, and then he loses his wife."

"He's pretty shut off when it comes to women. I should know, half the unmarried staff at the school asks about him all the time. What's he like? Does he date? I think if he ever wanted a relationship, he wouldn't have any trouble."

"That's too bad, you know? Shutting himself off like that."

"Is it?" Julie eyed her suspiciously. Her eyebrow arched in true detective style.

"What? Of course it is."

"I don't know, Taye. You and Coop have so much history together."

She shook her head. "It would never work. Besides, I think he barely tolerates me."

"Oh, I don't know about that."

Taylor peered out the window and saw Coop on bended knee speaking with his daughter, thoroughly engaging her in conversation. Taylor couldn't hear what he was saying, but there was no mistaking the love between the two of them or the hero worship in Cassie's eyes. Coop was meant to be a father, and she had no doubt he was a very good one.

"You can't take your eyes off of him," Julie said.

She gave her cousin a withering look. Was she serious? "Julie, do you want me to march my way back to New York on foot?"

"You know I don't want you to leave. Ever."

Taylor shrugged. "You're impossible."

"But you love me."

"Like a bratty older sister."

"I'm only older by two months."

"And I never let you forget it."

COOP HAD MIXED feelings about tearing down the gazebo. It held some really good memories for him. He'd spent a lot of time in this backyard, playing with the girls. They'd been a threesome, until one day in his seventeenth year it dawned on him that waiting for summer to arrive hadn't just meant no school or homework or getting up early. It meant Taylor. Seeing her after a long separation, being with her during those hot, sultry Texas evenings, holding her hand, kissing her. He'd fallen hard for her, his heart open and bursting with love. It pained him that he'd had to work with his dad part-time that last summer, but it only resulted in his time with Taylor being more precious, more valuable. And they'd made every second count.

Now, his crew was ripping down that part of his past and hauling it away.

"Cassie, you be careful with that. Those planks have nails in them," he called to her as she struggled with a partially full wheelbarrow.

"Okay, Daddy," she called back.

He couldn't resist smiling. She was determined, and strong, the beautiful result of the powerful love he had with Francine. Her memory, her spirit was always with him, reminding him how fragile life was. How one moment, he was doing something as mundane as deciding what to have for dinner, chicken or pork chops, and the next, a horrendous car crash takes her life. Francine had been vital and young and she hadn't deserved what happened to her.

Her death was a shock, a blow that destroyed him. It had been his fault and he would always live with that guilt. After Francine passed away in the hospital, he'd had to break the news to Cassie. He'd had to tell her the unfair news that her mommy hadn't survived the accident. She'd hung on for days but she just didn't have any strength left. He'd had to tell his little girl her mommy wasn't going to tuck her in at night. She wouldn't be there for any more dinners, or baseball games, or school concerts. She wouldn't be there to see her graduate from college or see her walk down the aisle at her wedding. It was a robbery, a cruel crime of events Coop had trouble dealing with, all the while trying to pretend to his daughter everything was going to be all right.

"Hey, boss," Toby said, walking over holding something in his hand. "I found something in the gazebo remains. You might want to take a look at it."

Coop came out of his thoughts to focus on what Toby was saying. "What's that?"

"It's a box of some sort, though it's pretty beat-up. Looks like it's handmade."

Coop immediately recognized the box. It was the one he'd built for Taylor after that summer they'd made up the promise game. It was supposed to be Taylor's treasure box, but they'd found it served a better purpose holding their yearly promises to each other. Those promises *had been* their treasures. They'd bonded them through the years. Julie had never wanted to participate in their game, and that'd been fine with them. Coop had crafted the box in his father's barn, home of Cooper Construction, and had etched their initials into the oak, TP and RC, and then stained it a walnut brown. It had been a source of pride to him and something just between him and Taylor.

Coop stared at it for a few seconds before Toby handed it over.

"Do you know what it is?" Toby asked.

"Yeah, I do. Did you open it?"

"No, sir."

"Fine. I'll take care of it. I know…who it belongs to. Thanks."

"Sure thing."

Toby walked off and Coop was left standing there, holding the box in his gloved hands. He'd wait all year long for summer to come, to see Taylor and compare their promises. Neither one of them had ever failed to keep their promise to each other. Coop loved the competition it represented, but it was more for Taylor. She was a staunch believer in keeping her promises. It was ingrained in her and to his knowledge, she'd never broken one.

But he'd forgotten about the box, putting it out of his mind over the years. It seemed like a lifetime ago now, twelve long years and countless events had happened since.

Cassie walked up, her gaze fixed on what he held in his hand. "What's that, Daddy?"

"Oh, uh, nothing. It's just an old box. It got dug up with the gazebo."

"Really? Can I see it?"

"Uh, sure. But don't open it." He handed it over carefully.

"Why not?" Cassie asked.

Because I don't want to see what's in it.

Because it had once meant a lot to me.

And because, if it was empty he wouldn't know if that was a good thing or a bad thing.

"It's not yours to open, Cassie. Remember how we respect other people's property."

"Okay," she said, disappointed. She turned the box over and inspected all sides, then handed it back to him. "It's just an old box anyway."

"Right," he said. "Hey, we're finishing up out here. Why don't you clean up and let Taylor know you're ready for her?"

"Daddy?"

"Yeah, Cass?"

"What's Taylor's last name?"

"Preston, why?"

She glanced at the box again, noting the carved initials, and smiled. "No reason."

Grimacing, he scratched the back of his neck as Cassie walked into the house. Sometimes, his daughter was just too doggone astute for an eight-year-old.

Coop marched over to his truck and set the box inside the glove compartment. He'd decide what to do with it later. Taylor had a right to it, but he wasn't ready to hand the box over.

He wasn't ready to lose one more thing from his past. Not just yet.

TAYLOR SET OUT her sewing box in the parlor, then grabbed her tape measure and notepad. She could make Cassie's flower girl dress with her eyes closed, but it'd been a while. The last time she'd designed a child's dress had been for Simone's little sis who'd needed something special for her solo piano performance. As Taylor recalled, the dress and the recital had been a hit. And now, here she was, years later, making one for Coop's eight-year-old daughter. This one would have to be just as special for Julie's wedding.

Cassie entered the room and parked herself right smack in the middle of the parlor.

"Are you ready?" Taylor asked.

The girl gazed at the sewing supplies curiously and nodded.

"Okay then, in order for me to make you the perfect dress, I need to take your measurements, so the dress fits you just right. But first of all, we need to take the hard hat off." Though she looked adorable in it, the hat was a distraction. The little girl stood steady as a rock, like a frozen statue. "And second of all, you can breathe, Cassie. Actually, you must breathe."

Cassie giggled and her smile came out, all toothy and

sweet.

Taylor smiled too. "Do you like working with your dad?"

Cassie nodded. "I get to if I get good grades and do all my homework."

"That seems fair."

"I'm saving up for a new baseball mitt. Daddy's going to pay for half and I'll pay for half. I should have enough by next week."

"Well, that's coming up pretty soon. I bet you're excited."

Cassie lowered her voice. "I am, but I'd work for Daddy even if he didn't pay me. It's fun."

"Okay, I won't tell."

Cassie grinned and Taylor saw so much of Coop in his daughter—the mischievous glow in her eyes and her rock-solid determination. "Thanks."

"Okay, here we go." Taylor lifted the hard hat off her head and set it on the sofa. She sat on her knees to get to Cassie's level, raised Cassie's arm, and used her battered but trusty measuring tape. "Let's see this great throwing arm I'm hearing so much about."

"I'm a leftie," Cassie said.

"Is that so?" Taylor jotted down the length and then measured her other arm.

"It's a good thing. Coach says lefties have an advantage if they pitch. It sorta messes up the batters. Everything is backward. And Coach says he'll teach me how when I'm older."

"I wouldn't have guessed that about lefties. I don't know a lot about baseball." She measured her shoulder width.

"You don't?"

Taylor shook her head. "Back home, in the city, I never had the time to learn. Would you believe I've never been to a baseball game?"

"Never?" Cassie's eyes opened wide, as if that was inconceivable.

"I'm afraid so." Taylor took measurements around her waist and then from her waist to her knees.

She was just about finished when Coop walked into the room. As Taylor looked up, their eyes met. A bunch of silly little nerves stole into her stomach sparking havoc. It happened to her every time he entered a room. Old habits died hard. Maybe that was it. Maybe she was just remembering the boy he'd been. The one she'd loved. Yet, he was different than the Coop she'd known and it had been years. So why was she noticing his tall broad frame, his muscular forearms and the sky blue of his eyes? Why was she glancing at his mouth and remembering the lush full kisses they'd once shared?

"Hey, Cass. I hope you're cooperating with Taylor."

"She is," Taylor said, rolling up her tape measure. "She did great. I think I have all I need. Cassie, I'm going to match the color of your dress to the other two bridesmaids, but it will be a little bit different in style. Would you like that?"

She shrugged. "I don't know. I guess so."

Taylor put her hand on Cassie's shoulder. "You'll do great and I might have to call you back for a fitting once or twice. That wouldn't be a problem, would it?"

"No." Cassie put her head down, deep in thought.

"And if you don't like something, you can tell me. Deal?"

Cassie nodded. "Deal."

"Okay, well, I'll let you two get on with your plans for today. Thank you, Cassie. I'll see you soon." She began gathering up her things, ready to head upstairs to start on the dress.

"Daddy, Taylor's never been to a baseball game," Cassie announced.

"Is that so, Cass?"

"It is," she said, shaking her head. "Never."

Coop raised his brows and gave her the same look Cassie had, as if she'd grown two heads or something. "Really?"

Taylor met his gaze. "Really."

"Well, maybe you will one day. There's still time. The season just started."

"You can come to my game, Taylor."

"Oh, uh..." She didn't quite have a comeback for that. Cassie caught her off guard.

"It's on Sunday," Cassie said. "At three o'clock. Right, Daddy?"

"Yes, but, Cass, Taylor probably has a hundred things to do for the wedding. I think she'd be too busy to come."

"You're not too busy, are you?" Cassie asked, hope radiating from her eyes.

"I, uh…" She looked at Coop, then back as his adorable daughter. Taylor didn't want to let the girl down. She didn't want to see pain in her eyes or disappointment. She'd probably had her share of that since losing her mother. "Sure, I can come. I'd love for my first baseball game to be with your team." She pumped her fist. "Go Tigers."

Cassie clapped her hands several times, her face beaming. "Promise?"

Taylor thought about it a second. "Yes, I can promise you that. I'll be there, Cassie."

"Yay! My daddy…I mean Coach says we always have to try our best, but I'll play extra hard. 'Cause it's your first game and all."

"I appreciate that, Cassie."

Coop handed his daughter her hard hat. "Why don't you wait for me in the truck, sweetheart? I'll be right out."

"Okay," she said and Coop kept his eyes on her until the front door closed behind her.

Then he turned his intense blue gaze on her. "It's nice of you to do all this for Cassie. But you don't have to come. Cassie will understand."

"I'll find time," she said, tilting her head as another thought entered her mind. "Unless you don't want me there?"

"Why wouldn't I want you there? I mean…it makes no difference to me if you come or not." He twisted his face. "That came out wrong. Look, all I'm saying is that you're not obligated to do anything for us."

"I know that," she snapped. "You're acting as if we weren't friends once."

"I'm not acting. We're not friends now. We don't know each other anymore."

"So, that erases everything in our past?"

"No, but—"

"But what? You're still blaming me for our breakup?"

He jerked his head back, as if she'd slapped him. Which, she wasn't going to lie, the thought did cross her mind.

"It has nothing to do with that. It's just Cassie. She's vulnerable and she gets things in her head sometimes. I don't want to see her hurt."

"I'd never hurt her, Ryan Cooper." She breathed the words out in a whisper, from the very depth of her soul. His accusation really stung. "Why would you think that?"

He took a deep breath and sighed. "I don't want her to get the wrong idea about the two of us."

"Us? Why would she? As far as she knows, we were once good friends."

Coop clamped his mouth shut, like he used to do when he knew a secret and wouldn't tell. Obviously, that trait stayed with him to adulthood. Something was up, but she wouldn't get it out of him, not judging by the stubborn set of his jaw.

"Coop?"

"What?"

"I'm going upstairs to work on Cassie's dress. Unless you have an objection to that?"

His mouth twisted. "No, no objection."

"Fine. Oh, and I *am* going to Cassie's game on Sunday. Because I promised her."

"Right and you never back out of a promise, do you?"

"Not if I can help it, no. Have a good day," she said sweetly, grabbing her sewing supplies and walking away. At the moment, she felt anything but sweetness toward him.

And when she got to her bedroom, she whipped her arm back and flung all her supplies onto the bed, her sewing kit hitting the wall with a thud.

Darn that man. Coop always could make her temper flare.

Chapter Five

SUNDAY MORNING, TAYLOR helped Julie make brunch for the female half of the wedding party. Her bridesmaids, Nicole and Lindsey, were seated outside on the patio as they all forked into quiche lorraine. Fresh berries along with salad and homemade lemon poppy seed muffins complemented the meal thanks to her and Julie's combined culinary talents. They'd had a blast cooking together and, in the end, the meal did turn out delicious.

Mimosa was the drink of choice and, after a couple of refills, all four of them were in a very giddy place.

"I can't wait for the wedding," Nicole, the kindergarten teacher, said. She was a longtime friend of Julie's. "Julie's the first of us to plan a wedding. She's our lab rat."

Taylor blinked, but Julie only giggled. "That's right. You're putting me out there on the front lines. Making me test the waters first."

"You've got a secret weapon, Jules. You've got your very own tailor, Taylor. Get it?"

"Good one," Lindsey said, chuckling. She was the music teacher at the school and apparently had a lovely singing voice. "I can't wait to see your wedding gown."

"Well, that's why we're all here, isn't it? To see how all the gowns fit."

"And I'm here, to *tailor* your gowns, if they need it," Taylor said, grinning. The champagne drink was definitely going to her head too.

More giggles.

"You and Lindsey aren't far behind," Julie added. "Summer will be here before you know it and then we'll all three be married."

"So, the three of you are engaged?" Taylor hadn't gotten the memo, not that she even had a prospect in the fiancé department.

She glanced at each one of the girls, suddenly feeling a bit left out. A tinge of envy swept through her, the feeling completely foreign. She'd never been envious before. And maybe she wasn't now, exactly. Maybe, she was just wondering what she was missing out on. It made her question her goals and priorities. She wasn't allowing herself a personal life, she was dead set on keeping the promise she'd made to her mother, to herself. While everyone else seemed to have both, a love life and a career.

"I'm getting married in July," Lindsey said, her voice elevating. A combo of nerves and excitement. "It's coming so quickly, I can hardly believe it."

"And my wedding is in September," Nicole added. "So much to do."

"I can imagine." She sighed and then remembered her manners. "Congratulations to both of you…actually, all of you."

Julie put a hand on her arm, looking at her far too seriously, an underlying question in her eyes. "Thanks, Taye."

She snapped out of it quickly. No need to worry her cousin. "Wow, those mimosas pack a punch. I'm gonna need strong coffee."

Julie bounced up. "Like mud?"

She nodded. "Like mud."

"I'll be right back."

And an hour later, after drinking a strong dark roast blend, Taylor was feeling herself again. That momentary bit of envy gone, she was back on track and sitting on the sofa with Julie. The two bridesmaids went first, coming into the parlor in true fashionista style, big smiles on their faces as they modeled their light rose chiffon gowns. The bodice was form-fitted with pale pink and white sequins, and the skirt flared from the waist. Perfect for a spring wedding.

Her maid of honor gown was of the same light rose coloring, but a bit different in style. Julie had wanted it that way, so Taylor had made variations to her gown.

"These look beautiful on you," she told the two bridesmaids, rising from her seat. "But I think, Lindsey, you'll need more of a hem if you plan to wear those shoes." She bent to tug on the hem and pin it in the right place. "The dress is dragging on the ground a bit. It'll get too dirty without a little adjustment."

"Okay. Thanks."

She walked over to the other bridesmaid. "And, Nicole, the waistline is a little baggy on you. I can take a tuck on the seam and tighten it up a bit." She demonstrated by cinching in the fabric and eyeing where she'd have to make the alteration, pinning it carefully. "It'll fit your frame just right. Just don't gain five pounds in the next two weeks, okay?"

Nicole snorted a laugh, feigning a horrified expression. "Gosh, if I do, just shoot me."

Taylor laughed too. "Okay, Julie. It's your turn. Time for the big reveal."

"Yes, we're dying to see your gown, Julie," Nicole said.

Julie rose and grabbed her hand. "I'm excited for you guys to see it too. But I need Taylor to get me into it."

And a few minutes later, they exited the bedroom and came down the stairs. Taylor took her seat on the sofa again to let Julie make her grand entrance. She was met by oohs and aahs, Nicole and Lindsey not shy about sharing their enthusiasm.

"I love it," Nicole said.

"Copy that, it's amazing. Julie, you look like a…I don't know, a princess with edge, a true statement of sweet and sass. It's definitely different, all those angles, they work. I wouldn't have guessed it," Lindsey said.

"And the way those pearls are sewn over your shoulder."

Julie beamed. It was clear she was thrilled her friends

liked the gown. "It was Taylor's idea. These are my mom's pearls and I really wanted to wear them on my wedding day, but the strand just didn't look right with the dress. You know what I mean? And then, Taylor performed a miracle."

"I'll say. It's unique."

"That's Taylor." Julie smiled her way. "Her designs are distinctive and definitely one of a kind."

"I guess I do think out of the box sometimes," Taylor said. "Maybe too far out of the box, ending up somewhere in unemployable land. Or else I'd have a job right now."

"I'd hire you in a heartbeat," Nicole said.

"Me too," Lindsey said.

"You ladies are very sweet," Taylor told them. She really did appreciate their support. It helped boost an ego that had been recently deflated. "But what's important is that the bride is happy. That's my goal when I design a gown."

"And you succeeded," Julie said, picking up the sides of her dress and twirling around like a fairy princess. The material spiraled around her body and flowed back into place as she finished her turn.

Everyone took a moment to stare at the glowing bride-to-be.

Then Lindsey piped up. "Taylor, have you ever...I mean, would you ever consider, oh never mind."

"What is it?" Taylor asked. "Would I ever consider what?"

"Well, I have a piece of my grandmother's veil that I

wanted close to me when I walk down the aisle. I know some people would have it wrapped around the bouquet stem, but I've been hoping to do something different with it. Though, I don't have a clue what and I wondered…"

"I'd be happy to take a look at it, Lindsey."

"You would?" Lindsey's pretty blue-gray eyes lit up. "Maybe you can help me come up with a better idea."

"Maybe I can."

"Gosh, thank you."

"You're welcome." Taylor didn't mind a challenge. And if, after giving it some thought, she couldn't help Lindsey find the perfect solution, she would be honest with her. But already her mind was working overtime with ideas.

Nicole bit her lip and glanced at Julie a few times. Julie kept nodding to her friend. Apparently, Nicole wanted to say something and Taylor waited, but then Taylor's cell phone rang. She smiled at the photo coming up on the screen. "Excuse me, I should probably get this." She walked out the back door and sat at the table where they'd had brunch.

"Simone! It's so good to hear from you."

"Good to hear your voice too. Tell me, how's it going in Last Stand?"

"Well, I'm still adjusting to being back here. It's been a long time, and it's certainly different than home, but Julie is keeping me busy. We were just finishing up a fitting when you called."

"Sounds like fun. I imagine you're wowing everyone with

your designs."

"Julie is pleased and that's all I care about right now."

"Oh yeah? What about the third side of your equilateral triangle?"

"My what?"

"You know, the guy. The one who was part of your Last Stand trio, every summer. The one you left behind. Have you seen him?"

"Coop? Uh, yes. I've seen him. He moved back here recently. His daughter is the flower girl in the wedding, actually."

"And?"

"And nothing, Little Miss Troublemaker. Nothing's going on. And why would it? Are you forgetting I'm leaving after the wedding?"

"Yeah, about that. Taylor, I've got some good news. Remember Swivel Bridal, the new cutting edge salon I was telling you about? Well, they'll be opening their doors next month and one of their new hires fell through. There's an opening. It might be perfect for you."

"Really?"

"Are you interested?"

Taylor thought about it for a moment. Was she ready to put herself out there again? To be judged? To have her designs scrutinized and go through marketing to see if they hit the right note with the buying public? She sighed. It certainly was her goal, and the promise she'd made to her mother was always in the back of her mind. She couldn't break that promise. She couldn't give up on her dream. "I...am. I'll send them my résumé when I get back."

"Maybe you should do it sooner, Taye. I don't know how long the position will be open."

"You're probably right. I'll look over my résumé. It needs an overhaul, but I don't know how much time I'll have to work on it. I promised to devote my time here to Julie and the wedding."

She wanted that. She wanted to continue on her "break." She was just beginning to feel like herself again. Beginning to unwind and gain some confidence again. She wasn't sure she could handle another rejection right now. Last Stand was her sanctuary, in heart and mind. Being here meant safety and friendship and family.

"Okay, but don't wait too long, hon. So, what's on the agenda for the rest of the day?"

"Well, believe it or not, I'm going to my first baseball game."

"You and...baseball? Well, it's about time? What team are you going to see?"

"Have you ever heard of the Tigers?"

"The Tigers? The *Detroit* Tigers?"

"There's a Detroit Tigers?" she asked.

"Are you kidding me? Haven't you ever heard of them?"

Taylor laughed at Simone's outrage. "No I haven't, but there is a Last Stand Tigers team made up of seven- to ten-year-old boys. Oh, and one girl. The flower girl, Cassie. She's got quite an arm, from what I'm told."

"Ah so, you'll be seeing her dad there."

"Of course. He's the coach."

"Maybe he'll teach you a thing or two about getting to first base again. He was your first kiss, wasn't he?"

Taylor shook her head. Her friend was relentless, but yes, Coop had been her first kiss and her first love. "Oh, look, it's almost time for me to go."

Simone's chuckle came across the wires. "Okay, okay. But be sure to let me know what's up. And if you want me to take a look at your résumé once it's done, shoot me a message. I'll be glad to."

"Thanks, sweetie. Will do. Stay out of trouble while I'm gone."

"I would say the same about you, but I know you too well."

"Ha, ha. Love ya."

"Love ya too."

A FEW HOURS later, Taylor walked toward the baseball field that sat at the edge of town, only a mile down the road from Julie's house. It was a good day for a walk, the sun shining overhead and marshmallow clouds dotting the spring sky. Her lungs were in shock by the freshness in the air, each inhalation easy, with no trace of smog. She wore a striped jersey and a Texas Rangers ball cap sat on her head, thanks to Julie.

"You have to do it up right for your first game," she'd said. And Taylor allowed Julie to dress her for the occasion. Turnaround was fair play.

As she came up to the grass field and dirt-lined bases, Coop was the first one she spotted. He stood out on the field, tall and broad, sporting a perpetual two-day-old beard that only highlighted his fine sharp bone structure. He'd grown into a beautiful man, yet dangerous to her psyche. He represented her childhood, the good times in her life, when things were simple and fun. And like Simone reminded, he also represented her first love. Girls didn't often forget that. And she hadn't.

As she approached, eyeing him on the field in a uniform that matched the team, her heart beat a bit harder, her breathing raced a little faster. She didn't particularly like the way he affected her.

Out of the blue, Cassie came running over. She looked like anyone else on the team, except for the cute smile and her blond braids. "You came!"

Taylor wanted to hug her but she didn't know how that would go over in a field full of boys, so she put up her hand and the girl high-fived her. "I sure did. I promised, didn't I? Are you ready for the game?"

"Yep, Coach is just about finished with warm-ups."

"Well, then I can't wait to see what all the fuss is about."

"Are Julie and Miguel coming too?"

"They'll be coming a little later."

Taylor looked up and found Coop approaching. Before he reached them, he gestured to his daughter. "Cassie, time to get with the team."

"Okay, Coach. I'll see you, Taylor."

"Sure, Cassie. Good luck."

Cassie ran off and Taylor stood staring at Coop.

He eyed her up and down. "Cute getup."

Heat rose up her cheeks. It was the last thing she'd expected from him. "Julie's doing. When in Rome." She shrugged, holding her tongue to keep from blurting his "getup" was definitely eye candy.

"Game's about to start. We're the home team." He pointed toward the bleachers. "That side."

"Thanks."

He stared at her just long enough to make her squirm, and then turned around and jogged back onto the field.

She squeezed her eyes closed, then sighed and made her way over to the bleachers. She was about to take a seat, when she heard her name called out from the top riser. "Taylor Preston."

She looked up and found Joe Cooper, Coop's dad, waving her over. "Come on up here, girl."

She grinned immediately and climbed over three rows to get to the top. "Mr. Cooper, it's so good to see you."

The older man rose and wrapped his burly arms around her, hugging her tight. "Good to see you too." He released her and patted the seat next to him and she sat. "You look the same as always, haven't aged a bit. What's it been, twelve years?"

"It has been that long. And you beat me to the punch. You're the one who hasn't aged. You look great."

"Retirement and granddaughter-ing agrees with me, I guess. How've you been, girl?"

She spent a few minutes catching him up to speed on her life in New York.

And then the game began.

Joe Cooper took it upon himself to lay out the basic rules of the game, but when he started to speak about game strategies, she got a bit confused. There were two men on base already and two outs. "So you mean the pitcher is deliberately trying to walk this batter, so he can get the next boy out?"

"That's right. The batter is a slugger. If they give him the chance to hit, he could score all the runs. So, Coop is loading up the bases, and then the last out can happen at any base."

"I see," she replied, though she really didn't. Why take the risk? What if the other batter hit a good ball?

The batter was walked, and the next batter up at base took a swing and missed. That was what Mr. Cooper called it. "A swing and a miss."

Cheers coming from the Tigers fans went up, feet stomping the aluminum risers vibrated through the entire bleachers and deafened the ears. Parents and siblings made up the gist of the boisterous fans on both sides of the field. And an announcer over a microphone called the game. Baseball in Last Stand was a big deal.

The pitched ball was hit, rolling at a swift clip toward first base. Cassie was there, blocking the ball with her knees and scooping it up from the ground. She rose quickly to throw the ball to the pitcher who'd run to first base to make the final out. It all happened so quickly, each one of the players doing their part. The inning was over. Cassie and the pitcher fist pumped and there were smiles all around as the Tigers headed to the dugout. Coop waited for them, giving each player a high five as they took their places on the bench.

The whole thing smacked of community and family and a sense of belonging that Taylor hadn't felt before. Not like this. There was more to baseball than just the game. Was it like this everywhere? Or was it just small-town camaraderie? Whatever it was, she felt great to be included. She could cheer for Cassie and Coop and the Tigers, even though some of the game was still a mystery to her.

"Don't worry, you'll get the hang of it," Joe said to her.

"I think I will, Mr. Cooper. I learn pretty fast on my feet. Especially with you as my baseball mentor."

"Taylor, call me Joe or Grandpa Joe. I answer to either these days. Okay?"

"Oh, okay. Sure," she said, giving him a smile.

He was the most down-to-earth man she knew. That hadn't changed. Joe Cooper set a high standard and was a good role model for his son.

And just as that thought crossed her mind, Coop, standing beside the dugout, turned his head and their eyes met. There was something different in his stare this time. He glanced at his dad sitting next to her and then looked into her eyes again. The connection sizzled down to her toes, a powerful force pulling her in. Her heart beat faster again, stirring up emotions that were just under the surface. Emotions she'd tamped down for years. Hidden. Buried. Locked away.

And then he smiled.

A killer.

One that stole her breath.

She smiled back, gave him a little wave.

He turned back to the game.

Cassie was up. That little girl held her own against a field of boys, standing at the plate, facing down her opponents. She was the epitome of girl power and pride, braids and all. Coop's body language said it too. He held himself a bit taller, puffing out his chest as he watched Cassie stand her ground.

And then there was a sharp crack of her bat and Cassie was off, running to first base, running to second base, the crowd in the stands standing up and cheering. Joe was up on his feet, and she joined him, cheering for Cassie, who'd beat out the throw at third base. Everyone in the stands high-fived each other. Joe turned to her and they too did the five-finger hand slap.

"Cassie's a natural," Taylor said.

"She is. She loves the game. Her first triple of the season," Joe announced.

Once Cassie caught her breath, she looked over at her dad and gave him a big, unabashed grin.

There was a moment of pure joy on Coop's expression, something just between him and his daughter that was sweet and genuine. Taylor melted a little bit, witnessing their bond.

"They're a pair," Joe said.

Taylor had to agree. "I can see that. They're lucky to have each other. And you," she added. The trio of Coopers was a three-generation family. They worked. The love between them was almost tangible and a sight to behold.

Coop swiveled his head just in time to find her staring at him. Her nerves rattled a bit, her insides jumbling all up and she bounded out of her seat. "I, uh, I smell buttered popcorn. I'll grab us a bag," she said. "Can I get you anything else from the snack shack?"

"You're going now? We're about to score," he said.

"I won't be but a minute," she said, glancing at the wooden hut serving as a snack bar where a popcorn machine was busy churning out puffed corn. "There's no line right now. I'll be back in a sec."

"Well, all right. But come back soon. You don't want to miss Cassie scoring a run at home base."

"I'll be quick."

Popcorn wasn't really what she wanted. What she wanted was not to be unnerved by the Tigers' coach. She didn't want to feel unexpected thrills every time Coop gave her a glance. She needed a distraction and popcorn seemed like the easy out.

She headed along the left field fence, eyeing Cassie, crouched, focused and ready to run, her helmet fitting her just like her hard hat—oversized and adorable. As Taylor was making her way to the snack area another blistering crack reached her ears. Shouts rang out from the bleachers and players, "Heads up!"

Whatever that meant.

A man coming toward her yelled, "Look out!"

She looked up just in time to see the ball firing down on her. Then a smack to the side of her head brought her to her knees. And the shock of the hit took her the rest of the way down.

"Damn it!" Coop's voice seemed to be coming from a faraway place and then nothing.

"TAYLOR! TAYLOR! WAKE up!"

Taylor opened her eyes slowly. She looked up, into a

blue haze, not sure what she was seeing, where she was. And then the fuzz cleared and she was able to focus. It was Coop. He was hunched over her, concern in his eyes. She tried to concentrate, tried to remember. She was on her way to the snack bar and out of the blue, literally, a ball came barreling down on her. As her memory returned, so did the pain. Her head pounded.

"Hey," Coop said softly, though there was no softness on his expression.

All she saw was worry and alarm. How did he get to her so fast? He must've hopped the fence and raced over.

"How're you feeling?"

A crowd had swarmed around them, but they circled clear of Coop. He was in charge apparently.

"Like I've been struck by lightning," she answered.

He nodded. "It's gonna be okay. Soon as I get you to the hospital. Have that head checked out." Someone handed him an ice pack. "This is gonna be cold. But it'll keep the swelling down. You're gonna have a nice bump."

He applied the ice pack, and the cold shot straight through her head.

"I don't need to go to the hospital." She hinged her body up, and was immediately sorry. Everything swam in her head. She glanced at Coop again, who had his hands on her arms, steadying her.

"Whoa, not so fast."

"I'll be fine," she said, not too convincingly.

"Maybe. Hopefully, but you need to get checked out. Think you can stand up?"

She gave a tiny nod. No sense jostling her achy head any more. "Yeah."

She stood with his help, but everything went fuzzy again and she swayed to one side.

"Yeah, I don't think so," Coop said and then she was being lifted in his arms. He cushioned her carefully, one arm under her knees and the other against her back. She had no choice but to hold on, wrapping her arm around his neck.

"Keep the ice pack on," he whispered to her.

"Okay." She held it steady.

"I'm taking you to the hospital."

Joe Cooper made it through the crowd, Cassie by his side. "Should I call 911?" he asked.

"No," she said immediately. "I'll be fine in a minute. Please?" she asked of Coop.

"No thanks, Dad. Just stay with Cassie."

"But your game…" she protested.

"Will go on. I've got an assistant coach. Now, just relax, close your eyes and I'll take care of it."

She did relax, as much as she could nestled against his chest, held in his capable strong arms. He carried her to his truck and gently guided her into the front passenger seat. The seat cushioned her bottom and she laid her head against the headrest. "This is embarrassing."

Coop came across her body, the scent of his lime soap

jostling her senses as he pulled her seat belt out and strapped her in. "More embarrassing than diving into your aunt Suzie's pool and losing your bathing suit top?"

"Gosh, you remember that?"

"What thirteen-year-old boy wouldn't?"

He gave her a look, inches from her face, his eyes sharp and gleaming with the slightest twinkle.

She sighed and his focus went to her mouth. They were close, unbearably so, but Coop lingered there, in the moment staring at her lips. Her breath caught and suddenly she forgot all about the ache in her head. She sighed deeply, her heart racing.

"But you fished it out of the pool and closed your eyes when you handed it to me," she said softly.

"I wasn't too smart back then," he teased.

"You rescued me then, and now you're doing it again."

"Force of habit, I guess."

She laid her hand on his cheek, looked into his eyes. "Thanks."

He swallowed and backed away as if she were on fire. "No problem." Then he closed her door and climbed into the driver's seat.

And they didn't speak the rest of the way to the hospital.

COOP SAT DOWN on his bed, leaned his forearms over his

knees, and ran his hands through his hair. He didn't want to feel the things he was feeling. He didn't want to allow any emotions to escape from where he kept them locked and hidden away. He was done feeling, done with that part of his life. And his life was good now, having crawled out from under a landslide of grief. He'd survived Francine's death. Though barely. And he still missed her. But he'd had to go on. He had a daughter that he loved to high heaven and she'd needed her father to fill in the voids in her life.

But seeing that ball come down on Taylor today worried the hell out of him and he'd let all rational sense fly out the window. He couldn't get to her fast enough. He couldn't allow anyone else to see to her injury. His heart had pounded like a jackhammer, and he'd raced to her, high-jumping over the fence to be by her side.

He couldn't bear to lose another… He closed his eyes. Oh man. *Don't think it, don't say it.*

He couldn't bear to lose *her.* Not Taylor. His feelings for her had never died. Not really and he'd just realized it as he carried her in his arms to his truck. As he breathed in the sweet scent of her, held her near and prayed she'd be okay. He cared for her. Even though she'd chosen her career over him. Even though she'd tossed away everything he'd wanted. She'd be going back to New York soon, and with her talent, she'd land on her feet. And he'd go on being Cassie's widower dad.

According to the emergency room doctor, she'd been

lucky the ball had only grazed her head. She'd have a bruise for a few days but should be fine. What a relief.

When Julie had shown up at the hospital, Coop hadn't argued about taking Taylor home. Though it was hard letting her go, it wasn't his place. They were just barely friends again and he had to remember that.

Coop sighed and glanced at his nightstand, flirting with temptation. It was only a few seconds before he gave in and pulled out his bedside drawer. Inside, he lifted out the promise box and held it in his hand, checking it out again. He ran a finger along the etched initials, RC and TP. He'd been so young then, and the quality of his workmanship made him smile. Not bad for a young kid. He'd worked darn hard on making this for Taylor. And after they'd declared it their promise box, his dad had taught him how to attach hinges and a flip latch onto it. The box had weathered years of isolation under that gazebo, long forgotten. Now he stared at it, wondering what Taylor's last promise was to him.

He scoffed. "Probably something lame." But he held on to the box, not ready to open it.

Not ready to have that part of his life over.

"Daddy?" Cassie came into the room dressed in her cozy pajamas. He set the box back into his nightstand and closed the drawer.

"What is it, Cass?"

Cassie put her head down, studying the floor. "How's Taylor?"

"She's going to be just fine. The hit wasn't as hard as it looked. She'll have a bruise for a few days, but that's all."

"That's good."

Coop knew when something was bothering his daughter. She stood there, quiet as a mouse.

He lifted her chin gently with his index finger until she met his eyes. "What's wrong?"

Tears pooled in her eyes. "It's my fault she got hurt."

Wow. He hadn't expected that. His daughter surprised him sometimes. Tough on the outside, but inside she was soft as a marshmallow. She had her mother's good heart.

"And what makes you think that?"

"I asked her to come to my game. If I didn't ask her, she wouldn't have come and gotten hurt." Cassie's lips quivered.

It hurt to see her lay the blame on herself, but he mustered up and told it like it was. "It's not your fault, Cass. You didn't make her agree to come. The decisions adults make are usually well thought out. If she didn't want to come, she wouldn't have. It's like if I asked you to pick up your toys outside, and you go running down the steps and trip, is it my fault you tripped and got hurt because I asked you to clean up?"

She shook her head. "No, but, Daddy, I heard you tell Grandpa Joe it was your fault that Mommy died. Because you sent her to the market for ice cream and she…she never came back."

Coop's breath caught in his throat. Everything stilled

inside as a slow burn began to slide down to his gut. He had no idea Cassie had overheard that conversation. He didn't voice his guilt often, but it was always there, just on the edge of his mind, batting him over the head to remind him if he ever found some peace. He'd blamed himself from day one and his child was motherless because of it.

If only he hadn't craved ice cream that day. If only she hadn't volunteered to get it for him. It was a cruel twist of fate that his love of ice cream would result in his wife's death.

He wrapped his hands gently around Cassie's arms, making direct eye contact with her sad blue eyes.

"And, Cass, you know what Grandpa said to me? Did you hear that?"

She shook her head. "I don't remember."

"He said that it was an accident. That it was nobody's fault. Grandpa said I shouldn't feel guilty about Mommy loving me enough to make me happy. And I…I try not to. I try to remember the good times we had with her. I listened to my father. Do you think you can listen to yours? About Taylor? It's not your fault. Taylor doesn't blame you."

"Are you sure?"

"I'm absolutely sure," he promised her.

He couldn't have her beating herself up when her heart had been in the right place.

"I guess Taylor didn't know what 'heads up' meant."

"She knows now." He knocked a fist to his head. "It was a hard lesson."

The frown on Cassie's face lifted. "I don't think she'll ever forget it, Daddy."

He wouldn't either. It could've been much worse for Taylor. "Probably not." He touched the very tip of her freckled nose. "Hey, I remember a time when someone caught the ball with her nose."

She giggled. "That was dumb. And it didn't feel good."

"Nah, you weren't dumb, but you learned a lesson that day too."

It had scared the stuffing out of him seeing that ball collide with her face. She'd fractured a bone in her nose and the doctor had said it would heal on its own. "But you've never made that mistake again. Now you use your mitt as your protection, not your face."

She giggled again.

"It's getting late, sweetheart. Are you feeling better now?"

She nodded.

"Good. Now off to bed." He kissed her forehead. "Love ya, Cass."

She wrapped her arms around his neck and squeezed tight. "Love you too, Daddy."

ON MONDAY MORNING, Taylor woke with a start, sharp pounding grating in her ears. She rose and walked over to the window, peeling the curtain back. Down below, the crew was already at it, hammering away at the foundation for the she-shed. The clamoring faded in her head as she spotted Coop, hard hat on his head, dressed in his work clothes, jeans and a chambray shirt, sleeves rolled up. Was there ever a more appealing man?

He'd held her in his arms on Sunday, carrying her away to safety after she'd been hit. He'd come to her rescue, hopping the fence to get to her, and she couldn't think of anyone she'd rather have save her. Though the whole thing had been totally embarrassing, Coop didn't make her feel like a fool. He'd made her feel safe and protected.

She kept her eyes on Coop as he picked up a hammer and began working along with his crew. Old tender feelings stirred in her belly. She really couldn't afford the way she was beginning to feel about him, but that didn't stop her from eyeballing him, thinking of the what-ifs, in her life. What if she hadn't broken up with him? What if they found a way to be together? What if she hadn't let the fear of failing her promises, ruin the life she could've had with him?

Her mother claimed it was puppy love, a summer of awakenings in her heart. What she felt for Coop was just a passing fancy. Her words. Her mom always claimed she was too young to know real love. Deep down, Taylor always felt it had been her mom's way of telling her to focus on her own dreams, to stay true to her course.

And she'd heeded her wishes.

But now, seeing Coop again, she wasn't entirely sure

she'd made the right decision.

She sighed and backed away from the window.

Turning around, she faced the dresser mirror. "Ugh." The bruise on her forehead screamed, "Hello! I'm here. You can run, but you can't hide."

It only hurt when she touched it, but boy, was it ugly.

Julie called up. "Taylor, breakfast."

She walked over to the doorway. "I'll be down in five."

Taylor took a quick shower and dressed in casual clothes, denim jeans and a cream blouse, then ran a brush through her hair. She found if she parted it to the side, the strands hid some of the lovely eggplant-colored wound. Luckily, most of the swelling was down.

One last glance in the mirror and she whispered, "As good as it's gonna get."

Then she made her way downstairs to the kitchen.

Julie was waiting, handing off a coffee mug to her as she entered the room.

"Thanks, but you didn't have to cook breakfast," Taylor said. "You know I'm fine with cereal or toast."

"I was in a cooking mood this morning. French toast and bacon for us. Then I've got to get to school. The kids are excited for the Bluebonnet Festival. Each classroom is doing a poster as an art project, so I'm going in a bit early to set it up. The theme this year is kindness."

"I like that. Sounds like fun. I'd always heard about the Last Stand festival."

"Well, this year you'll be here to see it in person."

"When is it?"

"Coming up this Saturday."

"Oh, so close to your wedding. Are you sure you have the time?"

"I'll make the time. It's important to the kids. And the whole town loves to get involved. You'll see."

They both sat down at the table and dug into the food. Julie munched on a piece of French toast as she glanced out the window. "Looks like Coop's gotten off to a good start this morning."

She nodded and bit into a crisp piece of bacon. "Yeah, I heard."

Julie laughed. "Sorry. He wanted to start earlier, but I told him seven was early enough."

"Smart move."

"It shouldn't take them too long."

"I'm teasing, Jules. You've been to my apartment in the city. You know how loud it gets, horns honking, trucks rumbling by, loud conversations going on in the building. Believe me, I can take some hammering in the morning. It's second nature to me."

"I'm glad it isn't too disturbing. I'm so excited about this. Coop's plans are right on and I know it's going to turn out great. Coop's good at what he does."

"I know. He'll make it perfect for you."

"He could be running a big company in Los Angeles, but

he came back here to give Cassie a better life."

"That makes him a good father."

"And a good person. He's dealt with a lot of heartache but he's managing."

"Maybe he's trying to move on." Taylor sipped her coffee.

"Yeah, maybe. I hope so. He's…"

"A catch?"

Julie chuckled. "You read my mind."

"I always could. And, well, it's hard not to notice him."

"Especially after he nearly broke speed records coming to your rescue."

"I thanked him for that."

"So, what are your plans for today?"

"I'll be putting on the finishing touches to your gown. And I've got Cassie's dress to work on too."

"I wanted to thank you for agreeing to help Lindsey out with her wedding dress."

"I hope I can come up with something for her."

"I have no doubt you will, coz." Julie glanced at her watch. "Uh-oh. Gotta run or I'll be late. Would you do me a favor? I made a full pot of coffee for the crew. Would you mind taking it out to them while it's hot? Oh, and maybe they'd like some of those muffins you made yesterday."

"I bet they would. Sure, no problem. I'll take care of it."

"Thanks. I'll see you later!"

"Bye, have a nice day."

After Julie left, Taylor fixed up a tray with coffee cups, sugar and creamer, and half a dozen muffins. She was just about to bring it outside when the kitchen door opened and Coop walked in. He looked even better close up, his blue eyes deep enough to swim in.

"Oh, hi."

"Morning," he said. "How are you?"

"Doing well, how about you?"

"Fine." He smiled. "Is Julie around? I have a question for her."

"No, she just left for school."

"All right, I guess it can wait."

"So, you're making progress on the shed, I see."

"You could say that. Getting the frame up and all."

"I...I was just getting ready to bring a tray out."

Coop took one look at the coffee and muffins and smiled. "Thanks, don't mind if I do." He grabbed a muffin, bit into it and groaned. "Oh, man. These are good. Did you make them?"

"I did."

"Was it a coincidence, or did you remember that carrot raisin is my favorite?"

"I, uh," she began, deciding on telling the truth. "Julie reminded me. I may have asked her."

He took a seat at the table and arched a brow. "May have?"

"Okay, I asked her."

His charming grin disabled her and she sat down beside him. She placed a coffee cup in front of him and took one for herself. "Well, then, I have confession to make too," he said. "I saw Julie leave just a minute ago. I came in here…to see you."

She didn't know how she felt about that, but her heart began to pound. And not just a little bit. "Well, that's honest."

"I always try to be."

"And why all this honesty?"

"Maybe because I smelled the muffins baking and it sort of lured me in."

"Good try. But I baked these yesterday. Last I checked, you can't smell day-old muffins."

He gave her an innocent look. "No?"

She shook her head and smiled.

"So, maybe I came in here to check on you." He leaned in real close, until she could see the ocean-blue rim around his eyes. He braced his elbow on the table and with two fingers, brushed several strands of hair away from her face. He did this ever so gently, his touch careful and precise.

As he took in her bruise, his eyes narrowed to fine slits as if he were in pain. "Nasty."

"It looks awful, but it's healing."

"Does it still hurt?"

"No. Not really."

He released a breath. "That's good."

He gazed into her eyes and lingered there. He held her mesmerized, so much emotion passing between them, so much desire. It was raw and scary and unexpected. And when he leaned in closer, his fingers in her hair, and glanced at her mouth, she couldn't move away, couldn't stop what was happening. He held her face carefully, his thumb circling her cheek. And then, his lips were on hers, softly, gently, the scent of sugar and coffee mingling between them.

It was a kiss from the past, a kiss with no future, but yet she didn't have the willpower to stop it, to put a halt to this craziness.

But Coop did. He ended the kiss and backed away, holding her gaze. "I…I shouldn't have done that."

His remorse put an ache in her heart. Was he remembering his dead wife? Was it guilt that pulled him away? And if she was so against letting him in again, why was she disappointed? "And yet you did."

He shrugged. "I was worried about you."

"Is that all it was?"

"Isn't that enough, Taylor?" His voice elevated.

"What do you mean?"

He scratched his head, his face twisting. "Oh wait, I almost forgot, this place was never enough for you. *I* was never enough for you, was I? Never mind. Don't answer that, I already know."

His chair scraped back, the noise echoing against the kitchen walls, and then he was up, grabbing the tray for his crew. “Don’t get up; I’ll take this to the guys.”

She rose in spite of his command. “Coop? Exactly who are you mad at? Me or yourself?”

He opened his mouth ready to let her have it, but then he clamped it shut and appeared thrown off a bit, as if he was confused. He shut his eyes for a second, shook his head and then walked off, leaving her standing there, stung by his kiss and his parting words.

She’d broken his heart, and he still resented her. And to add insult to injury, he probably felt terrible pangs of guilt about his wife.

Maybe he was mad at both of them.

And maybe, just maybe, she was mad at herself as well.

For enjoying that kiss a little too much.

Chapter Six

TAYLOR WENT OUT of her way to keep busy, to keep from thinking about Coop and the way he'd kissed her earlier. It was a swift kiss, but no less passionate than when they'd been teens. Familiar and new all at the same time, he still had the ability to stop her heart with one brush of the lips.

She sighed and continued working on Julie's dress. The entire living room area was littered with her patterns and materials. The delicate work she was doing now required hand-stitching, so she turned up the radio and sat down on the sofa to apply sequins and individual pearls to Julie's dress. The pearls tied into the strand she was using for the shoulder strap and brought the entire look together. It was intricate work and as her eyes tired, she moved on to sewing Cassie's dress.

By midafternoon, she heard the guys outside packing up their gear. She'd glanced out the window a few times to see the progress they were making, she told herself. And there she'd find Coop, working alongside his crew, laboring as hard as they were. The skeletal frame of the shed now had wooden walls. It was starting to take shape and wouldn't Julie be thrilled when she came home today to see that?

There was a knock on the back door and she rose from the sewing machine to answer it. She had a suspicion who it was and she braced herself. As she opened the door, she found Coop there, hard hat in hand, a serious expression on his face.

"Hi," she said.

She hadn't been wrong.

"Hi, uh...Taylor. Do you have a minute?"

She opened the door wider. "Sure, come in."

He looked away for a second as if struggling with something. "It's a beautiful day. Take a walk with me. Please?"

Please? Of course she couldn't refuse him, not after the look on his face, the plea in his voice.

"Okay. Give me a sec."

"I'll meet you out front."

She closed the door and tidied up the living room, putting away most of her materials and closing up her sewing box. She put the gown on a satin hanger meant just for wedding gowns and took it up to her room, on the off chance that Miguel would come over in the next few minutes and see Julie's gown. After that, she took a brush to her hair, put on her tennis shoes, gave herself one glance in the mirror and then dashed downstairs. She peeked into the living room to make sure Muffy, who'd been sound asleep on a sunny patch of floor by the living room window, hadn't woken up.

The coast was clear. She stepped out the front door and found Coop waiting with his thumbs tucked into his front pockets, trading his hard hat in for a tan Stetson, leaning against the house like some authentic cowboy. It was so Coop, so Texan, like a scene out of a Western movie. One didn't see too many cowboy carpenters in New York. She grinned at the absurd thought and met Coop with a big smile on her face.

He began walking down the street. Each parcel in this part of town was on large lots with good-sized ranch homes. He walked in the opposite direction of his home, which was around the corner and then some, and she fell in step next to him.

"You're smiling," he said. "I didn't think you'd be happy to see me again."

"Maybe I'm smiling about something else."

"Are you?"

"In a way. I was thinking about how there aren't any cowboy carpenters in New York."

"So, you took one look at me and thought that?"

"If the shoe fits, Coop."

He ran a hand down his face and smiled too. "I guess so."

They strolled quietly for a while and then he cleared his throat and turned toward her. "Taylor, I want to apologize about before."

"You mean, when you kissed me?"

"Yeah, that too. But I shouldn't have spoken to you that way. I guess the kiss threw me, and I didn't know what to do about it. I mean, I haven't had to deal with those kinds of feelings..." He stopped and put his head down. "I haven't so much as kissed a woman since my wife passed. And then you come back to town. You're not even here a week, after years of separation and..." he said, shrugging, his eyes filled with turmoil. "It kinda got to me, you know?"

"I get it. We have history."

"Yeah, we do," he said softly.

"It was a long time ago."

"It was, and we're grown-ups now."

"That *is* the rumor," she said.

He shot her a smile and sighed. "It's just that..."

"You feel guilty."

Self-imposed blame reached his eyes, the grief he still felt for his wife. He must've loved her a lot. Since leaving Last Stand, she'd never experienced anything close to that sort of love. She had no one to blame but herself for the lack of romance in her life. She had a vision and a promise to keep, which meant staying focused and not letting anyone in. She'd pushed men away, nice men who'd offered her a relationship. But she'd never wanted that. Her ambition was sharp, focused on building her career and building great walls around her heart. Still, Coop had found someone, he'd found love again, and he had a wonderful daughter to show for it.

Taylor didn't even have a job.

Coop's head tilted to the left as he explained further. "It's Cassie too. I have to watch out for her."

Taylor put her hand on his arm. He was solid there, from years of physical labor. He was solid all the way around, a good, decent man who'd been dealt a bad hand and was struggling to make the best of it. "Always, that's a given, Coop. You're a wonderful father."

"Sometimes I wonder."

"No need to wonder. Anyone who sees the two of you together can see your bond."

"Thanks. She's a special kid."

"She is."

They began walking again, taking the direction leading to a giant oak tree off the shoulder of the road. A wooden rope swing hung from one thick branch. "Hey, would you look at that? The swing's still up. I can't believe it," she said. "How many times did we race to see who'd get to swing first?"

"Dozens."

"Yeah, you used to beat me all of the time. Until I got older, and then I'd outrace you."

Coop threw his head back and laughed. "Okay, if you say so."

"What? I did beat you, Ryan Cooper! Are you saying I didn't?"

His brows rose skeptically. "I'm not saying a word."

Taylor sucked in a breath. "You're not implying you let me beat you, are you?"

"Maybe, only one way to find out."

She pointed at his chest. "You wanna race now?"

"I'll give you a head start."

"For goodness' sake, we're living in the twenty-first century. I don't need a head start."

"Have it your way."

"On your mark, get set, go!" Taylor took off in a rush, leaving Coop a bit stunned. She was a New Yorker where she seized the moment. She didn't hesitate. She had to be on her toes to keep pace with fast city living.

"You want to be that way about it," he called to her, his footsteps just behind her.

She'd always been fast, and her morning jogs gave her the endurance she needed to pull off a win. She'd show Coop up and wipe the smug look off his face. He wasn't going to best her.

Her hair flew in her face, blinding her for a second, and then she glanced sideways and there was Coop, running right next to her, a big, silly grin on his face, as if he was playing her, as if he could beat her by five lengths if he wanted to. The swing was mere yards away, her strides eating the ground. She was in high gear now, her heart beating, her legs burning as she pulled away from Coop, leaving him half a length behind.

She turned to see him slowing, his eyes on her, as he deliberately put on the brakes. She reached the swing first, grabbing the rope and twirling the swing around. Coop was a second behind her and as their eyes met, the truth dawned on her.

She pushed at his chest and inertia had him backing up a step. "You did let me win."

"Always," Coop admitted.

"Why?"

He gave her a you-must-be-kidding look. "Why?"

"Yeah, why?"

"I was crazy about you, Taylor."

She kinda melted then, all her exasperation spent. She'd been crazy about him too. But neither of them had acted upon it until her last summer here. She sat her butt down on the swing and Coop took a place at the oak's trunk, leaning back watching her swing back and forth.

"I have good memories of this place."

"So do I," he admitted.

"So why'd you leave?"

"Same reason you did. Only I went to college on the west coast. And after I met Francine, I decided to stay and try my hand at the business end of building. I worked at a large construction company and was on my way up. We were happy, Taye. We had a good life and after Cassie came along, I didn't think my life could get any better. But then..."

She stopped swinging to stare at him.

He squinted, as if remembering painful memories. "Things don't always work out the way you think…you know?"

She nodded. "I do know. I didn't expect my mom to die so young. I never knew my heart could hurt so very much. And Dad hasn't been the same since."

Coop inhaled. "I'm sorry about your mom."

"And I'm sorry about your wife. Truly, Coop."

"I know you are. We could always talk, you and me."

She smiled. "That's true. And remember those promises we would always make to each other? I think the hardest one for me was when I promised you I'd learn how to ride a horse. In New York? I think I was about twelve and I drove my mom crazy until she finally took me to the country. I had a two-hour private lesson and, you know, I did learn. I can saddle up a horse if I had to and ride Western, single rein. But the truth is I never got the chance to ride a horse again."

"Well, you're in horse country now. You could always refresh your memory."

"I don't know," she said, hesitating. "Maybe one day." Her gifts were with a needle and thread, not in a saddle. "What was the hardest promise you made to me? Or don't you remember?"

Coop looked away, and his expression seemed to sour. As if the subject made him uncomfortable.

He inhaled and focused back on her. "I remember, Taylor. Those promises meant a lot to you."

"Wonder what ever happened to—"

"It was definitely when I promised you I'd grow a beard," he rushed out. "I don't know why I agreed to that. I was sixteen and I remember the guys at school giving me grief for the slim excuse of facial hair growing in peach patches on my face." He gave his head a shake. "But damn if I didn't do it anyway."

"I remember. You sent me pictures. I think I still have them."

"Burn them. Please."

She grinned and leaned way back on the swing. "I will not." She pumped her legs and began swinging again, Coop watching her as she flew through the air, back and forth, back and forth. After a minute, she took one last full flying swing. Then she dropped her legs, dragging her shoes across the ground to stop and get off.

Smiling and fully exhilarated, she offered Coop the rope. "Your turn."

He stared at her a good long moment, something stirring in his eyes. Something that made him change his mind about swinging. "I'm…good," he said. "I, uh, think we should head back. All this reminiscing is making me hungry. My dad's probably got something decent cooking on the stove."

She studied him a second, unsure of his abrupt change of heart. "So, Joe's a good cook?" she asked.

"I didn't say that. He's just better at it than I am. And poor Cass, she doesn't stand a chance."

"Well, I could teach her a thing or two in the kitchen while I'm here. If you think she'd like that."

"She definitely would, but I don't think so. You're doing enough already, making her flower girl dress."

"Yeah, about that. I'm gonna need Cassie to come by for a fitting in a day or two."

"That's not a problem. I'll have my dad bring her by Julie's after school. Just text me when you need her."

"Okay, I will."

"Let's head back."

He nodded toward Julie's house and dark strands of hair fell across his forehead, bringing a warm ripple of awareness to her chest. She wanted to run her hand through the thick mop and put the strands back in place, or mess it up even more. She wanted to touch his cheek, look deeply into his eyes, kiss him.

She was getting familiar with his moves again, the gestures she'd memorized from one summer to another. His deadly smile, the light in his eyes when something intrigued him, the look on his face when she'd walk into a room. Was she imagining that? Or was it real?

She'd be a fool to fall for him again.

She wanted to promise herself she wouldn't.

But that just might be one promise she couldn't keep.

COOP CLIMBED DOWN from the cab of his truck and walked toward the back door of the home he'd grown up in. He'd lived the first seventeen years of his life in Last Stand, and then returned only a year ago to pick up where his father left off with Cooper Construction. Things just sort of fit, actually, better than he'd imagined. He was happy with his work and Cassie was happy with the friends she'd made here. This was a better life for her. She loved Last Stand and she loved living with her grandpa Joe. Coop had done the right thing by moving back.

So why the heck was he feeling so doggone restless all of a sudden?

Had to be Taylor.

She reminded him of his youth, the summers that went unequalled. The fun they'd had. Seeing her again brought it all back, and wasn't he acting like a young fool around her? Hiding the promise box from her. Gosh, why hadn't he told her today that he'd found it? Why was he hanging on to it? Refusing to look inside?

And why on earth did he kiss her today? Sure, he'd been worried about her. Seeing that awful bruise on her forehead had gnawed at him. He hated seeing her hurt. And then she'd gazed up at him with her pretty green eyes, and he was a goner.

He'd always been a sucker for Taylor, but kissing her had come out of left field.

"Daddy!" Cassie came running out of the workshop and

raced into his arms.

He lifted her up and twirled her around. "Hi, Cass." He kissed the top of her head and set her down. "How was school today?"

"Good. I got one hundred percent on my spelling pre-test. And now I don't have to take the real test!"

"Awesome, Cass." He put up his hand and she high-fived him.

"And we're working on a poster for the Bluebonnet Parade."

"That sounds like fun."

"Every class gets to do one."

"What's this I see?" He turned her arms over and found blue and yellow smudges. "Last I recall, the paint's supposed to go on the poster, not your arms."

She giggled. "I know, Daddy. I'm just not as neat as you and Grandpa."

He winked at her. "You're neater than us in other ways. You pick up your clothes without me having to ask. And you put your dirty dishes in the sink. And you make your bed much better than I make mine. So see, you are neat. Besides, when I was your age, I'd have twice as much paint on me than you did. Maybe three times as much."

"Really?"

"Really. Hey, how would you like to stop by Julie's house tomorrow after school?"

"Can I help you with the shed?"

"Well, maybe. But first, Taylor needs to see you. She's gonna make the prettiest dress for you and she needs you to try it on."

Cassie put her head down. "Okay."

"Hey, I told you she doesn't blame you for anything. In fact, she's excited to see you again."

She poked her head up. "Really?"

"Yes, she thinks you're pretty special. But then, I already knew that."

Cassie punched him in the arm, a pretty good slug. "You have to say that, 'cause you're my dad."

"Ow, girl. Save that slugging for the batter's box. And, yeah, I guess I have to say it, but it doesn't make it any less true. C'mon, let's go in and see what Grandpa's got cooking on the stove."

"Are you hungry…as a tiger?"

His eyes widened. Cassie loved playing this game. "You know I am." He grabbed Cassie around the middle and lifted her up. She kicked her legs out and laughed her head off as he tickled her. "I've caught me a pretty delicious tiger right here, just in case Grandpa's meal isn't up to snuff, I'll gobble her up."

"No, no, you can't do that!" Cassie giggled like crazy. "You'll…lose your very best…first baseman."

Her laughter filled his heart. There was not a better sound on earth.

"Oh yeah," he said, finally putting her down. "Can't do

that. I need the star Tiger of the team."

Cassie nodded, bobbing her head up and down, and then marched into the house with a wide grin on her face.

"THIS IS VERY nice of you, Taye," Julie said again as they got into her car.

They were off to Lindsey's apartment to take a look at her wedding gown.

"It's not a problem. I have the time. Everything is going smoothly here and I don't mind helping her out if I can."

"But you haven't had time to work on your résumé and there's that job opportunity that sounds perfect for you."

It did sound perfect for her, but she was dragging her feet and she wasn't sure why that was exactly. Was she afraid of failing again? Losing her job had made her gun shy, but she'd never been one to give up. She'd always found a way to achieve her goals. So, was she simply burnt out? Maybe she really needed this time to regain her confidence and unclutter her mind. "I know you're right. I probably should clean up my résumé and send it out. I just… I don't know, I feel a bit off right now."

"Off? How?"

"I'm not sure. Maybe I just need this vacation."

"Vacation? You've been working since you got here."

"Doing what I love to do. So, it doesn't really count as

work."

Julie pulled up to an apartment building in town and parked the car. "Well, here we are. Lindsey is thrilled you're coming over."

"I don't want to get her hopes up."

"Just be honest. That's all you can do."

They got out of the car and walked through the high Spanish archway of the building. The motif and open-air layout of the two-story apartment complex was so different than the multistory walkup apartments where she lived in the city.

Julie led her to Lindsey's second floor apartment and knocked. She opened the door right away, a big smile on her face. "Hi, girls! Come in, please. Thanks so much for coming, Taylor."

"I'm happy to do it."

"I have wine and chocolate for us. I hope you don't mind but I invited Nicole to join us. Thought we'd have a little impromptu wedding-party party."

"Are you kidding? This is great. It's Miguel's turn for poker night. He's having a guys' night and so, it's only fair, we have a girls' night."

"I'm game," Taylor said. It gave her one more excuse not to work on her résumé.

Nicole walked out of the kitchen, carrying a tray of assorted cheese and crackers. "I brought snacks too."

"Nicole, good to see you again," Taylor said. "And

thanks for this."

Julie echoed her comment. "Yes, thanks for everything, you guys." She gave both the girls a hug. "You treat us so well."

"So, what first?" Lindsey asked. "Want some wine?"

Taylor piped up. "I think I'd like to see your gown first. Before the vino goes to my head. Is that okay with everyone?"

The girls all nodded. "Okay, we'll put the wine on hold," Lindsey said. "I'm kind of nervous and excited about this anyway. Should I try the dress on for you?"

All three girls chorused, "Yes!"

And then they all laughed.

"Have a seat, you two. Nicole, would you mind helping me?"

"Not at all," Nicole replied.

She and Lindsey stepped into the bedroom while Taylor and Julie took a seat. Minutes later, Lindsey walked, or rather *flowed* into the living room, showing off her gown. "This is it," she said, barely containing her joy. There was just something about a woman in an ivory wedding dress that made her feel like a princess.

"Stunning," Taylor said. "I love the cap sleeves and the sweetheart neckline. The satin suits you."

"It's truly beautiful, Lindsey," Julie added.

Nicole held a large piece of a wedding veil in her hands. "I agree, of course. Lindsey, you look amazing. Maybe

Taylor can figure out how to add your grandmother's veil in."

"Yes, what do you think?" she asked, handing her the voile and lace material. "It's been ripped, that's why I only have half of it. So it's useless as a veil, but I wanted to keep my grandmother's memory alive somehow."

Taylor studied the piece, looking at it and then at Lindsey's dress. She sat quietly for a moment, three pairs of expectant eyes watching her. Her mind began churning out ideas, one after another, and once she'd exhausted her supply, she closed her eyes envisioning the dress with her best option. "Okay, I have an idea, but it requires cutting most of the veil. Lindsey, your dress is simple in design, the folds of gorgeous satin making the key statement, so if we added a little something to it, it wouldn't be an eyesore and the veil is just ivory enough for it to work. How would you feel if I made an underlay of your grandmother's veil around your cap sleeves? I could stitch it from underneath and either pleat or drape it, depending on what you'd prefer. You'd see an inch all the way around. And if you like that idea, I might just have enough material left over to do the same around the hem of your dress. It would have to be hand stitched as well, but I think I could do it. Here, let me show you."

Taylor demonstrated her idea, using the material and walking Lindsey over to the hallway mirror, showing her how the sleeve would look. "What do you think?"

"I think...yes! I would love that." Tears welled in Lindsey's eyes and she reached over to give Taylor a big hug. "Thank you. This is very," she said, her voice breaking, "important to me. So, yes, to the sleeves and the hem."

"Well, then," Nicole said. "Now that it's all settled, it's time for wine and chocolate."

"That's right," Lindsey said. "Give me a minute to change and we'll have our party. In Taylor's honor."

"Me?" She pointed to herself.

All three of the girls looked at her with hero worship. She wouldn't lie, it felt good. Real good.

THE NEXT MORNING, Taylor rose early, donned a pair of running shorts and a T-shirt that read "Designers Do It with Style" and then took off jogging. Last night, she imbibed a bit too much pinot and lost all sense of willpower gobbling down dark chocolate truffles like they were the last ones on earth. She woke feeling bloated and all around icky. Now, she was in full redemption mode, promising her body a healthier day. Water would be the drink of the day. And black coffee.

Morning sunshine beat down to warm her bones and she pushed her sunglasses onto her nose as she began to jog along the sidewalk, Coop's warning ringing in her ears. This time she headed toward town drinking in the puffy-cloud sky and fresh morning air as she jogged along Main Street. She was feeling better already, her stomach unclenching and her head clearing. As she neared Char Pie, the local pie house, the sound of a truck's engine purred behind her, its presence on the street giving her pause enough to glance back. There she found a red truck slowing, matching her strides, and its owner behind the wheel wearing a wide grin.

Coop stuck his head out of the window partly. "I see you're taking my advice. Sidewalk running."

"Have to. Rumor has it there's a crazy truck driver on the road. And he stalks joggers."

"Stalks?" He laughed like it was the funniest thing he'd ever heard.

She laughed too. It was a pretty outrageous statement and she stopped in her tracks. She was feeling too good about her progress to let Coop ruin her day.

He parked his truck on the street in front of her and got out.

"What are you doing here?"

"You mean, aside from stalking you?" His smile could charm the devil.

She gave her head a tilt, trying to ward off the butterflies flapping around in her tummy. "So, you admit it."

"I'll never tell." Then he pointed to the shop. "Actually, I'm picking up turnovers for the guys. Hump day and all. Thought I'd grab a coffee while I'm here. Join me?"

She pushed the strands of hair that had loosened from her ponytail off her face. "I'm a mess. I can't go in there."

"You're not a mess. You look…more than fine."

The scrutiny he gave her muzzled any response. The way he said "more than fine" birthed more butterflies. Was he actually giving her a sweet compliment? "Come on, I hate to drink alone."

She sighed and went along with his request. It was easier than coming up with more excuses. "Okay, I guess I could take a break."

He gave her a triumphant smile and put his hand to her lower back and ushered her inside the shop before she could change her mind. "This okay?" he asked, pulling out a chair at a two-seat café table.

"Sure, it's more than fine," she repeated, returning his smile.

"You're in a good mood," he said as she sat down.

"You sound surprised."

"Is Texas finally growing on you?" He sat facing her.

"I've always loved Texas, you know that."

"Yeah I do. It's a great place to visit, but you'd never want to live here, kind of thing."

"Coop."

"Teasing, Taylor. It's what I do."

She wasn't so sure he was, but she let it go. "So how was poker night?"

"You know about that?"

"I can stalk too, you know." She pursed her lips.

He arched his brows. "Ah, Julie told you. Poker was

good. Beers with the guys is always fun even if Miguel won last night. How was your night with the girls?"

"I'm afraid too much vino for me. And I broke the bank on chocolate truffles. So here I am, jogging it off. Or at least trying to."

"What will you have?"

"Just water for me, please. I need to hydrate."

"Gotcha. Give me a sec to order, I'll be right back." He rose and headed to the counter.

She waited for him, wondering if they could ever just be friends again. Wondering if they could overlook the love they'd once shared and regain their friendship. She'd always valued him, always thought of him and Julie as her besties. But that had been her summer life. Not the real thing.

"Hey, where did your smile go?" he said, sitting down and handing her a glass of water. "You look like you're doing some heavy thinking?"

"Nope, not really." She wasn't going to bring it up. She didn't want to go there. "Thanks," she said, taking a few swigs of water. "This is just what I need."

He tasted his coffee. "And this is just what I need." But he was looking at her the entire time. His blue eyes were like a magnet, drawing her in, crowding her stomach with flutters.

"So, how far do you run usually?"

"I try for four miles. Sometimes I end up walking the last half mile. I'm not in the best shape."

Again, his brows rose.

"Hey, I'm not fishing for a compliment or anything."

"Still, Taye...you're too hard on yourself. From where I'm sitting, you're in damn good shape."

Heat moved up her neck. The way he was looking at her and his compliment rattled her nerves. Since when did Coop make her so nervous? Her mind flashed to that last summer when her emotions went crazy and her heart sang only one song. For Coop. "Thanks. Maybe I should get going..." She pushed her chair out and was ready to stand, when Coop touched her arm. The slight touch sizzled all the way up to her shoulder.

"Stay a little while longer. I have something to tell you."

She inhaled a sharp breath.

"It's about Cassie."

Oh, good. Cassie was a safe subject. She didn't think she could handle anything more from Coop right now. Her feelings were in a jumble. She liked him, had always liked him, and those feelings were getting stronger.

"What about Cassie?" she asked, lowering down in the chair.

Coop focused on her forehead, and the bruise that was finally starting to fade. "She really likes you."

"And I really like her too."

Coop smiled. "She acts tough, but inside she's a marshmallow. Soft and sweet."

Where was he going with this?

"Cass got it in her head that she was to blame for you getting hurt at the ball field. She thinks if she hadn't invited you, you wouldn't have gotten injured."

"Oh, no. Well, that's not the case at all."

"I explained that to her and I think she understands, but since you're seeing her today for the fitting and all, I thought you should know."

"Thank you. I'm glad you told me. I'll be sure to keep that in mind when we talk. She's really a nice young girl, Coop. Not that I have any experience with raising a child, but I can tell you've done a good job with her."

"Pop and I, we try. Still, it's not the same as having a mother and Francine was so good with her." He sighed, pain entering his eyes for a moment. "So, what about you? Do you want children one day?"

"Me? Uh...yes. One day, maybe."

"You mean there's no boyfriends waiting for you back home?"

She chuckled at the thought. "Boyfriends? As in more than one? I haven't had a date in over a year, so I'd say they're not lining up behind my door or anything."

"That's hard to believe, Taye."

"Not really. I don't meet a lot of new people in my line of work."

"And you're too busy to get out there and mingle."

"Something like that. Honestly, now that I'm jobless, I'll be searching for work, once I get back." She had a résumé to revise sooner rather than later. Or Simone would be all over her.

"I have a feeling you'll land on your feet."

She gave her head a tilt. "Why?"

He shrugged. "Because that's what you do. Remember the time you and Julie tried to surprise both of your moms with the perfect peach pie?"

"Don't remind me. I was in charge of making the crust and I totally blew it. First, I undercooked it, then I overcooked it and burnt the edges. And when I finally thought I mastered the perfect golden brown crust, the bottom turned out to be a soggy mess."

"Yes, and I benefited from your blunder. I got to eat the mess-ups."

"You called me Soggy Bottoms for the rest of that summer."

"I was such a—"

"Jerk?"

His lips twitched and he shook his head. "I was going to say I was such an inspiration to you."

He was so not going to say that. He was a tease. Always had been. "What are you talking about?" Her voice rose as she chuckled at the absurdity. "An inspiration?"

"Don't you remember? I made you promise me you wouldn't give up until you got it just right."

"Oh yeah, I do remember that now."

"The very next peach pie you tried to make on your own

was perfection. When you promise to get it done, you don't stop until you do, Taylor. I've always admired that about you."

"I'd had enough practice. After a while, you make all the mistakes you're going to make, until one day, it all clicks. Of course, I wouldn't have succeeded without you *inspiring* me."

He scrubbed his jaw a few times, eyeing her boldly. "Glad you recognize that." He smiled, a destroyer, and this time when she rose from the table, he didn't try to stop her. Thank goodness.

"Off to the races again," she said.

He rose quickly too. "I'll see you later."

Oh, right, at Julie's. She couldn't quite get away from spending time with him. "I'll remember what you told me about Cassie."

"Thanks. She's in good hands with you."

Her chest puffed out a little bit. It was a compliment she wouldn't question. Coop had a way about him that was sort of...irresistible. Wow. What was going on inside her head these days?

Nothing good, it seemed.

Chapter Seven

"HERE YOU GO, Cassie." Taylor lifted the flower girl dress to the little girl wearing a T-shirt and ripped jeans. The sewing machine and her supplies were taking up residence in Julie's dining room. "How do you like it?"

It was the same shade of pink as the bridesmaid dresses, but with a few more ruffles and lace added. Taylor loved working on this dress, but Cassie was showing little enthusiasm.

"It's pretty," she said finally.

Muffy was at her feet, wagging her tail, waiting for recognition. Not even the cute pup could pry a smile out of Cassie.

"Why don't you go into the bathroom and try it on. Then I'll see if I need to make alterations."

"Okay." She marched away, head down.

"Let me know if you need any help," Taylor called after she heard the door click shut. Then she focused on the pup, picking her up and tucking her close to her chest. Muffy wasn't used to being ignored. "Come here, Muff." Taylor stroked her under the chin and ran her hands through her fluffy fur. She whispered softly, "Something's wrong with our little friend. I think we need to find out what it is, don't you?" She set Muffy down and the pup circled an area in the corner of the room a few times before lying down, chin on her paws.

And a minute later, Cassie stepped out of the bathroom, the dress hanging off her shoulders.

"Here, let me zip you up in the back."

Cassie turned around and Taylor zipped her up. "There, better. Don't you look pretty," she said, guiding her around to face her.

Cassie shrugged. "I guess so."

Taylor studied the dress from all angles. "Looks good, but I think it might need a little tuck at the waist. I think the length is just fine."

Cassie didn't say a word.

"Hey, I wanted to thank you for inviting me to the baseball game the other day," Taylor said. She hadn't planned on bringing it up, but apparently something was still bothering Cassie and she wanted to ease her mind. "I really enjoyed it. Grandpa Joe taught me a little about the game."

"But you got hurt," Cassie said, stealing a quick glance at her fading bruise.

"Just a little bit and it doesn't hurt at all. It was my own fault. I should've paid more attention when people shouted 'heads up.' Next time, I'll be more careful, that's if you're willing to invite me again."

Cassie gave her a slight smile. "Sure. We have a game next week."

"And I'll try to come. Would you like that?"

Cassie nodded.

"Wonderful then. Be sure to tell me when, okay?"

"I will."

"Now it's time for me to get to work. It'll just take a few minutes."

She put her hands upon Cassie's shoulders and spun her around. "Here, hold completely still. I'm going to put a few pins where I need to tighten up the waist a bit."

Taylor concentrated on pinning her, feeling Cassie's tension come through the material of the dress. There seemed to be something more bothering Cassie and she hadn't a clue what it could be.

"Cassie, don't you like the dress?"

"I…do." She practically spit the words out and then put her head down.

"Are you sure?"

"It's just that…"

"Do you want to be a flower girl?"

"I thought I did. And Julie is so nice to me. But…" She shrugged, obviously struggling with something.

"But what, honey?" Taylor looked her in the eye, trying to assure her. "You can tell me."

She was ready to accept anything Coop's daughter had to say.

Cassie teared up, her eyes filling with moisture. "I don't wear dresses ever. People will laugh at me when they see me in this."

Stunned, Taylor didn't know what to say initially. And she chose her words wisely. "I know you are more comfortable in your jeans and play clothes, so am I. But sometimes, we have to dress up for special occasions. Julie and Miguel's wedding will be a special day, right?"

"Yes."

"And you know everyone there will also be all dressed up?"

She nodded.

"Cassie, you do look very nice in this dress. Very flower-girlie and I think you'll surprise some people in a very good way when they see you wearing this."

Her eyes brightened. "You do?"

"Yes, I really do. And you know what my mama told me when I was about your age and feeling embarrassed about performing a dance in my ballet recital? She told me it doesn't matter what the rest of the world thinks, just so long as you hold close to your heart the ones who really love you. And I happen to know many people love you, Cassie. Can I show you something?" she asked.

Cassie nodded and Taylor pulled out the heart-shaped locket she kept tucked underneath her blouse. "My mama died some years ago and when I get to feeling a little bit scared or unsure, I remember my mom is always near, and it gives me courage. See," she said, pressing the latch and opening the locket to expose a photo of her mom holding her as a baby. She's here with me. I've been wearing it every day since I left New York."

"It's pretty," Cassie said. "My mom died too. When I was five."

"I know, and she's someone you hold close to your heart, right?"

"Yes."

"Cassie, maybe you have something that gives you courage. Can you think of anything? And it can't be your baseball mitt."

Giggles rose up from Cassie's throat and the sound swept straight through her. At least she could make the little girl laugh.

"I know that," Cassie replied.

"It should be something special that you could wear or hold on the wedding day. Something that will give you super flower girl powers."

A thought struck and her eyes grew wide. "My daddy has a necklace that was my mommy's. He says I can wear it when I get older. He takes it out and lets me hold it sometimes. It's a heart too, with rubies around one diamond."

"It sounds very beautiful."

"It is. The prettiest thing I've ever seen."

"Well then, I think your daddy would surely allow you to wear it on Julie and Miguel's special day. Do you think that would give you strength?"

"I think so. If Daddy lets me wear it."

"Would you like me to ask him?"

She smiled and nodded. "Yes."

"Then I will."

Joy entered Cassie's eyes. Then she lurched forward and wrapped her arms around Taylor's waist. The hug was unexpected and loving and so surprising, it took Taylor a second to recognize what was happening. But that didn't stop tears from pooling in her eyes as she returned the hug with a big squeeze.

Coop was right, Cassie was a special kid.

With super flower girl powers.

COOP WAS PLEASED with the progress on the she-shed. The siding was up, and the windows would be going in after that. This was one of the easiest projects he'd engaged in, but it was also very special and he wanted everything just right for Julie. She'd been a dear friend all these years. And he and Miguel had become instant buddies when they'd first met.

Coop walked around the entire building, checking out the workmanship. As he rounded the corner and glanced at Julie's back door, he spotted Cassie coming out, a big smile on her face. She was eating a cookie, and Taylor was behind her holding a tray. The women of the house always made sure the crew was well-hydrated. This time, it looked like icy cold lemonade. He didn't know which was more appealing after a hard workday, the lemonade or the woman delivering it.

Taylor had a big smile on her face too and it was impossible for him to pry his eyes away.

"Take a picture, boss. It'll last longer." The oldest and most experienced of his crew, Toby Greene, was too damn observant.

Coop didn't like getting caught. Was he that obvious? And so what if he was? "I'm looking at my daughter, bub."

"If you say so." Toby grinned and began whistling a tune.

Coop sent him a warning glare, before returning to his inspection.

"Hi, Daddy." Cass came up beside him, hard hat sitting low on her forehead.

"Hi, Cass. Looks like you scored a big cookie."

"Taylor said only if it was okay with you. And I told her it was."

"Did you now?"

She nodded and took another big bite of her cookie. "It's okay, right?"

He chuckled at his daughter. The cookie was three quarters of the way gone already. He put his hands on his hips. "And what if I said it wasn't?"

"It's my after-school treat, Daddy. You never say no to

that."

The kid was right. He didn't deny her much. He cut her a lot of slack, as long as it was harmless. Out of guilt. Because she was motherless. It hurt in his gut every time he thought about it.

"And how was school today?"

"Pretty good. I beat Manny Lopez in a relay race."

"I bet that was fun. Were you a good sport about it?"

"I guess so. I told him he was fast too."

"That's my girl. Is Grandpa Joe here?"

"Nope, he dropped me off after he spoke to Taylor."

That brought his gaze back to Taylor, sitting at the patio table, speaking on her cell phone. She seemed animated, laughing with someone on the other end.

"And did all go well with the dress fitting?"

"Yes, but, uh, Taylor has something to ask you."

"She does? Looks like she's busy now."

Cassie glanced over at the patio table too. "She's talking to Blake Charles. I heard her say it was sweet of him to call."

"Sweet, huh?" Something pinged inside, a flash of emotion he wasn't used to feeling. Blake had had the biggest crush on Taylor in those final summers. He'd been a bit shy with Taylor and had never really gotten up the nerve to say much to her, but his big moony eyes told another story. They followed her around, dogging her every move. Coop had never really liked the guy. Now he owned and operated Charles Realty, a surprisingly successful business in the county. Taylor sure seemed to be enjoying herself talking to him, her laughter spilling over to irritate his ears.

Coop removed his hard hat and ran his hand through his hair. He took a kerchief out of his back pocket and wiped at his face a few times.

"Daddy, can I help?'

"If you want to clean up some of this siding, you know where the wheelbarrow is."

"Clean up, again?" she droned.

"I'm afraid you're too late to do anything else today."

"It's okay. I'll do it."

"Thatta girl."

Coop stuffed his kerchief away and noticed that Taylor was off the phone. He walked over to the patio table. "Lemonade looks good."

"Have one," she said. "They're for you and the crew."

"Thanks." He grabbed one and took a sip. "Mmm, best lemonade in five counties." Coop would always give the same compliment to Julie's mom.

Taylor smiled. "Aunt Suzie loved when you told her that."

He nodded and took another sip. "Are you busy? I noticed you on the phone."

"No, not busy. I was just talking to an old friend."

"Blake Charles?"

"How did you…oh, Cassie must've overheard."

"So, how is old Blake?"

"Old Blake?" She chuckled. "He's your age. And he's doing fine. I bumped into him at Java Time the other day. We had coffee together."

"Oh, yeah?"

"Yeah."

She clamped her mouth shut then. Had old Blake finally asked Taylor out on a date? Coop took a deep breath, reminding himself it was none of his business what Taylor did in her private life, yet the pangs inside weren't going away.

"Actually, Coop. If you have a minute, I do have something I want to ask you. Can you meet me in the kitchen? I'll take these lemonades over to your crew."

"Sure, I'll see you inside."

Coop entered the house and finished his lemonade, placing the glass in the dishwasher. Julie's home had been like a second home to him, especially during the summers. And when he'd returned to Last Stand, Julie made sure to tell him nothing had changed. Their friendship had picked up where they'd left off and that was another reason he was glad he'd come back to Texas. The town had embraced him and his daughter. But seeing Taylor again put him off balance. He didn't like it, not one bit.

Taylor entered the room with a brilliant smile on her face. "Thanks for waiting. I think we only have a minute or two before Cassie comes in."

"This is about Cass?"

"Well, yes. I could tell something was bothering her and with a little coaxing I was able to find out what it was. Apparently, she's embarrassed about wearing the flower girl dress. She thinks people will laugh at her since she's known around town as a tomboy. She told me she doesn't wear dresses. Ever."

"Wow." Coop sucked in a breath. All this was news to him and it caught him off guard, a sucker punch to his gut. How had he not figured this out on his own? "I had no idea. So that's what's gotten into her. Every time I mention her being in the wedding, she clams up."

"I don't think it's all that bad. She just needs something to give her a bit of courage. Something to make her feel strong and comfortable. When I explained how wearing my mother's necklace gives me strength," Taylor said, drawing his eyes to the gold locket around her neck she was touching tenderly, "she told me her mom had a special necklace, but she wasn't sure she was allowed to wear it."

"Gosh, if it helps, of course she can wear it." Coop shook his head. He wasn't going to give the necklace to Cassie until she turned sixteen, but if it would make her more confident, it was all hers. "I think this is all my fault. I didn't realize I was doing my daughter a disservice. I didn't think it mattered that she didn't wear dresses or want fancy things. I had no idea she was feeling self-conscious. I should've known. She never puts a dress on. She probably doesn't have one that fits anymore."

"Coop," Taylor said, reaching out to touch his arm. The slight caress went deep to comfort him and ease his doubt. "Cassie is who Cassie is. You didn't do anything wrong. Her mother died, and you and your father have done your very best with her."

"I don't know."

"Trust me, I know. All girls go through something like this. They get embarrassed, they get shy, they feel unsure. Women are complicated beings."

Coop couldn't believe she admitted that and he chuckled. "Man, you're good, Taylor. Very good."

"I made you smile, didn't I?"

Their eyes met and held for a long moment. "You always could."

Taylor blinked a few times. There was history between them that couldn't be denied or forgotten. Coop was feeling it more and more. "Thank you for this, Taylor. I was clueless and you helped to open my eyes."

"That's another thing us women are good at," she replied, flashing him a sugary sweet grin.

He scratched his head and wondered what other clues he was missing when it came to Cassie. "I guess so." Still, he was uncertain.

"Don't beat yourself up, Coop. Most men are in the same boat. You haven't done anything to ruin Cassie's life. If you ask me, she's well-grounded and happy."

Taylor pushed her hair up and away from her face in an

absentminded way, not realizing how pretty all those glossy dark strands looked falling back into place. Coop's throat hitched a bit. Being around Taylor again was affecting him. In a good way and he didn't want it to end. She made him feel good about himself, easing his doubts and, well, just being Taylor. "Have dinner with me tomorrow night."

"Wh-what?"

Her green eyes grew wide. Apparently, he had the power to open her eyes too. "I think you heard me. I'm asking you out for dinner."

"Like…a…date?"

Hell no. Yes. "Think of it as two people sharing a meal together."

"Why?"

"Because, first of all, you've been great with Cassie, making her dress, giving her pep talks. Clueing her father in on all things female and, secondly, because you want to."

Taylor put a finger to her chest. "Me? I want to? How would you know that?"

"I just do. You love food, and this place has the best."

Taylor thought about it for half a second. "Sounds too good to pass up, okay."

Okay? Man, he hated how thrilled he was that she agreed. It scared him silly. "Okay, then. Dinner, tomorrow night, seven p.m."

"Yes." She smiled.

He smiled back.

And just like that, he had a date with Taylor Preston.

Wonder what Blake Charles would say about that.

Coop walked out of the kitchen, wondering if he knew what the hell he was doing.

And more importantly, why he was doing it.

TAYLOR LOOKED AT her reflection in Julie's hall mirror. She must've changed her clothes half a dozen times before settling on a solid cinnamon red dress with a V-neck, cinched at the waist only to flare out some. Maybe she should've opted for something more casual. Something that wouldn't give him the wrong impression.

Julie came up beside her and glanced in the mirror. "You look amazing."

She made a face, wrinkling her nose. "It's too much, isn't it?"

"No way. It's perfect."

"But I only agreed to this dinner because it seemed important to him to thank me. He was beating himself up about his fathering skills. And I—"

"You want to go, Taylor. Otherwise, you wouldn't give a fig about how you're dressed. Just go with Coop and have fun. I think this is your first date, in what, a year?"

Just hearing the word *date* in the same breath as *Coop* put her nerves on edge. "I'm not going to think of it as a date.

We're just two old friends having a meal."

"Okay, use whatever device you need to make yourself feel comfortable. But promise me you'll take it one step at a time and see where the evening leads."

Taylor nibbled on her lower lip. "One step at a time? Sure, I can promise you that."

"Good, because once Coop takes a look at you in that dress, you'll knock his boots off."

Goose bumps climbed up her arms. "It *is* too much. Do I have time to change?"

The doorbell rang.

Julie grinned. "Nope." She kissed her cheek and then vamoosed, as they said in Texas.

Taylor gave herself a talking to. This was no big deal. A friendly meal and an early night. That would be it. With that in mind, she opened the door to find Coop standing at the threshold. He swept his gaze over her, raised his brows as approval lit on his expression. In that moment, she was totally grateful she hadn't changed out of this dress.

Coop stood tall and handsome as ever, clean shaven but for the shadowy scruff along his jaw that was just enough to make him look dashing. His smiling sea blue eyes didn't hurt the look either. Add in a pair of black slacks, a snap-down tan shirt under a dark sports jacket, topped off with a felt hat, and she had one rather mesmerizing Ryan Cooper, cowboy style. Coop may be a contractor, but he was pure Texan through and through.

"You look very nice," he said.

"Thanks, so do you."

"Are you ready?"

She grabbed a black clutch purse from the hallway table. "Now I am."

Coop pressed his hand to the small of her back and guided her to his car. Every time he touched her, warmth traveled through her veins and a sense of longing she'd shoved to the back of her mind emerged. "Where's your truck?"

"Not here, that's for sure. I figured you'd be more comfortable in Dad's SUV."

"That was thoughtful, but I'm okay in a truck."

Coop smiled as he opened the door for her. "Not in that dress, you're not."

The compliment was in his tone, rather than his choice of words, and it felt really nice hearing it. Maybe she really did need a night out.

He got in the car and started the engine. "The last time I picked you up in a dress, you were wearing a frilly wedding gown. Looked like a fish out of water. With all the flopping around you were doing."

So much for his compliments. "Gee, thanks. What a visual."

He grinned like the devil he was and pulled away from the curb. "You know what I mean."

"Sorry, next time maybe I should let Muffy get completely lost."

"I had no trouble getting her to mind."

Darn if he wasn't right. Muffy was a cuddle muffin and a sweetheart, but she never listened to her. The darn pup had a mind of her own when it came to obeying.

"So far, there've been no more escapes, so it's all good."

Her cell phone rang and she dug into her purse to look at the screen. Coop glanced down at the same time, noting the name. It was Blake. Good manners let the call go to voice mail. She wasn't one to ignore a friend to speak to someone on the phone. Unless it was urgent.

"Blake again?" Coop said matter-of-factly. "That guy's persistent."

"He is not persistent about anything personal. It's business, sort of."

"Oh yeah? What's business, sort of?"

"It means his baby sister is getting married and he's buying her wedding gown. He wants it to be something special and asked if I could show them some of my designs. Give them some tips."

"A likely story." Coop wasn't buying it at all, but he was good-natured about it and why shouldn't he be? Just because he was taking her to dinner didn't mean she couldn't spend time with other friends in Last Stand. "What guy goes wedding gown shopping?"

"Oh, you'd be surprised. Fathers, cousins, besties and, yes, brothers. For some, the wedding is a family affair. After all, a girl only gets married once." Then she added, "For the first time, that is."

Coop's mouth turned down for a second in a move of disapproval or…? No, she wasn't going to go there.

"Is that so?"

"It's a fact."

"Gotta be good for your business then. All these people buying wedding gowns."

"Actually, it can be lucrative in big cities like New York, but honestly, I'm surprised at how much interest there is in Last Stand. I mean the town has lots of appeal, like a shabby chic version of old town America, but—"

"A what?"

"Don't tell me a builder of your status doesn't know what shabby chic is?"

"Of course I know. I am building a she-shed for Julie, remember? Just never thought of the town as being considered that way."

"Well, when you think of it, Last Stand is timeworn, but stylish. Longstanding but trendy and fashionable. And the festivals around here are known throughout the state."

"Yeah?"

"Yeah, people enjoy the traditions without feeling behind the times. It's kinda cool how novel and charming the town really is."

"You sound like a spokesperson for the place."

"You know I've always liked this town."

Coop held back his next comment. She could see it in his

eyes and on his expression. And she didn't want to rehash her reasons for leaving and breaking his heart. He knew them all too well. It was a can of worms she didn't want to reopen.

She'd promised Julie she would give this evening a chance. But was she right to promise something like that? Did she hold too fast to her promises, regardless of the outcome? Being here in Last Stand gave her freedom to debate that in her head. Had her promises led her astray at times?

It was a short drive to the restaurant and once Coop parked the SUV, he told her to wait and then came around to the passenger side and opened the door for her. Southern manners were not wasted on her. She liked the gentlemanly act and wondered if it would become a lost art soon. Sure, she was perfectly capable of opening the door for herself, but it was those little nuances that men did that made a woman feel extra special.

At least it did for her. "Thank you," she said, accepting his hand as she exited the car.

But the hand-holding ended there. Coop released her and tension immediately drained out of her body. He led her to the entrance of the Dragonfly with the slightest touch to her back and a hostess greeted them. They'd gone on a few real dates when they were seventeen, all that a working Coop could afford, and those times were easy and fun. Honestly, back then, they hadn't cared if it was a burger joint or a coffee shop, as long as they were together. They'd never gone to any place remotely as nice as this restaurant.

They walked along tumbled stone and were shown to a table for two in the garden. Uneven brick walls created an outdoor terrace flourishing with plants and flowers. Rich in rustic elegance, the place hit just the right tone for the evening. Coop pulled out the chair for her and she took a seat. He sat facing her and gave her a smile.

"This is really nice, Coop."

He looked around the place. "Yeah, the food's good too. I've taken Cassie here on special occasions."

"Such as?"

"Her seventh birthday. Honestly though, she would've been happier with a hot dog and a cupcake."

"Most kids would."

"When we were younger, I would've given anything to take you to a place like this." He sighed. "I don't know why I just said that."

"Maybe because it's true?"

"It is, but that was another lifetime ago."

"Still, you're a part of my best memories, Coop. We can't think back and not remember all the summers we spent together with Julie."

"I know you're right. I can't get it out of my head."

"What?"

"That you're here again. I know it's only temporary. But at least we've had a chance to reconnect."

"Reconnect?" Taylor's heart skipped a beat. What was he

trying to say?

"I mean, we're adults now. We've both been through loss and a lot of time has passed. So I thought maybe we could try to be friends again."

"Friends?" Oh, man, he was pulling the friend card.

The hope swelling inside her chest just deflated. What had she wanted him to say? She didn't know exactly, but she'd never stopped being his friend.

"I think we are, Coop. At least on my end."

He pulled back a second. "On your end? You never answered my letters. You never picked up the phone when I called."

"I know. I'm sorry about that. Truly, but it was hard enough leaving and I thought you'd be better off not hearing from me."

"So you did it for my sake?"

"I did."

He shot her a skeptical look just as the waiter came by to deliver the menus and take their drink order. Coop ordered a bottle of cabernet and then picked up the menu.

She did the same. "What do you recommend?" she asked to break the silence. Apparently, Coop still had issues with their breakup.

"It's farm to table so everything is fresh and delicious."

The menu was extensive and everything looked mouthwatering. Her stomach growled and she quickly gazed at Coop. If he heard, he didn't react about it. She was fully expecting him to tease her. Funny, but she never minded his teasing. It was part of who they once were.

"The spinach salad sounds yummy."

"So is the Dragonfly special," he said. "It's the chef's own creation. Chicken fried steak, carrot souffle, topped with a vegetable medley and any choice of potato."

"That sounds delish too."

Coop closed his menu. "Done."

She liked his decisiveness. He certainly knew how to impress a girl. He seemed at ease in this situation, while her heart was pounding hard. Because it was easy for her too. Being with him made it seem like no time had passed at all, and that sort of freaked her out.

"What's wrong?" he asked, sensing her mood.

"Nothing really. Just wondering if this is what it would've been like if we hadn't broken up. If we dated as adults. It all seems so…"

"Natural?"

She bobbed her head. "Yes."

Music coming from a three-piece band began playing from the other side of the garden. The tunes were mellow and soft, lending an atmosphere for romance. This entire evening was surreal, and she could get lost in it, if she weren't careful. The truth was, she hadn't been on a date this nice in years, but she'd be fooling herself to think that was all it was. It wasn't lack of a social life drawing her to Coop.

A woman in a white chef's coat came over to the table.

"How are you, Coop?"

Coop rose and greeted the woman. "Delilah, it's good to see you." He gave her a hug and then turned to Taylor. "Delilah Corbyn, I'd like you to meet Taylor Preston. Delilah's the chef and owner of the Dragonfly."

"Nice to meet you," Taylor said.

"Same to you. I hope you find everything to your liking here at Dragonfly. After your meal, I'll send over a special dessert for you both."

"That'd be real nice. Thank you," he said.

"Do you have any questions about the menu? Is there anything I can do for you?"

"Not at all. We're both having your special. You know how much I like it."

"Good choice. Well, I'd better get back to the kitchen. Enjoy your meal."

"I'm sure we will," Taylor said.

After she walked away, Taylor asked, "A friend of yours?"

"She is, I suppose. I've done some work on this place. Helped her out of a jam when her contractor messed up on a renovation."

The waiter came by with their wine, opening the bottle and pouring it for them. Then he took their order.

Afterward, Coop held his goblet up. "To friends," he said.

Taylor clinked her glass to his. "To friends."

They looked over their glasses and sipped wine together.

"Mmm, it's delicious."

Coop kept his eyes trained on hers. "It is."

A shiver ran down her spine. Was he flirting with her? After all their talks, he was sending mixed signals and driving her crazy. Didn't he just say in his last breath he wanted to be her *friend*?

During dinner, Taylor managed to steer the conversation to Julie's she-shed. Coop explained about the two rooms inside, with an open air feeling so that she didn't feel closed in. One room, separated only by a wall partition, would be her library where she could sit and read comfortably, the other one would be a craft room. It was going smoothly, which Taylor could tell. She complimented his work and they moved on to Cassie and how she was doing at Honeysuckle Elementary.

"It was a hard transition for her, leaving her school friends, coming to a new town, only to start first grade here in Last Stand. I remember feeling helpless and having to give her freedom to be sad and lonely. It was the hardest thing, seeing Cassie hurt and not being able to make it right for her. Luckily, my dad was the voice of reason. He helped both of us adjust."

"I'm sorry you two had to go through that." Her heart ached for them.

"You know what? Tonight's not about the past. Let's not dredge it up." He rose from the table and offered her his hand. "Dance with me?"

Baffled by his offer, she glanced around. She'd been so deep in conversation with him, she hadn't noticed other couples were up and dancing to an upbeat tune. She took his hand and rose, taking his lead, ready for a quick dance on the garden lit floor. And just as she faced him, the song ended and another slower ballad took its place. They stared at each other for a second, then Coop shrugged and drew her up close. She placed her hands on his broad shoulders and he took her waist.

They moved slowly, in step with each other, swaying to the music, getting lost in it. There was no awkwardness or reluctance, just a natural fit. For her, it was the prom she'd never gone to with him, the spring flings and parties they'd never attended together. Coop's hand moved up her back, drawing her closer, and she flowed into him willingly, relishing the moment, remembering the past and enjoying the present.

She breathed in fresh soap and lime aftershave and her senses came alive. Tingled.

"You smell like strawberries and cream," he said softly in her ear.

She chuckled and admitted, "I was just going to say I like your aftershave."

"I'll remember that."

"So will I," she murmured.

He stopped dancing and studied her, his eyes soft and gleaming, and her breath caught in her throat. She couldn't look away from his striking gaze. She couldn't deny something was happening between them that was more than friendship. Then he drew her up close again and they fell back in step with the music.

"You're a good dancer," she whispered.

"It's easy with you in my…with you. I've missed you."

"I've missed you too."

They'd been apart for twelve years, but it didn't feel like that now. It felt like they were right back where they'd started from. And it was exciting and comfortable, which was hard to figure. She was feeling all sorts of emotions. Mostly good ones.

The sun clung to the last vestiges of light, creating a golden blast on the horizon, the music surrounding them soulful and romantic, and instinctively they moved closer to each other. She laid her head on his shoulder, breathed in his scent, and her eyes slowly closed.

He cupped the nape of her neck and whispered, "Taylor."

When she lifted her head to gaze at him, his mouth came down on hers, softly, gently, and she closed her eyes, absorbing every wonderful sensation she was feeling. It was a beautiful kiss, a lovely meeting of the lips. Right there on the dance floor, Taylor realized how much Ryan Cooper meant to her.

The music ended and he released her, but the bond was still there, in the smile on his face, the gleam in his eyes. She wanted to say something. Ask him if that kiss meant anything to him. Ask him if he felt the same way about her as she felt about him. But the words wouldn't come, her throat dry with fear. Was she insane to hope? To attach any credence to what had just happened between them. Or was it simply a kiss?

Turmoil entered Coop's eyes, a mixture of pain and confusion. As if he hadn't planned on kissing her. As if he just now realized what he'd done. He took her hand and led her back to the table. They both took their seats.

"Maybe we should have dessert now."

"I thought I just had some." She tilted her head, unable to resist teasing him. Anything to remove the regret singeing his eyes.

"Yeah, about that…"

"Shh. You don't have to say anything, Coop. In fact, it's better that you don't." She knew the drill.

They didn't need to rehash their past or try to compensate for it. They didn't have to try to make sense of an impossible future. At least she'd kept her promise to Julie. She'd given the evening a chance. And look where that had gotten her.

"Tell me all about this Bluebonnet Festival coming up on Saturday?"

Clearly relieved, Coop went on to explain about the festival and parade, a Last Stand tradition that celebrated bluebonnets and the onset of spring. But as he spoke, she only pretended to listen, concentrating her thoughts on hiding a heart that was beginning to break.

Later that night, while in the confines of her bedroom, she opened her computer and began revamping her résumé. Back in the real world, she needed a job. She couldn't let the romance of small-town life deflect her from her goals. Never before this determined, she worked into the wee hours of the night and then emailed the final draft to Simone for editing and review.

At least now, she was making a move toward her future.

Coop or no Coop, there'd be no more languishing in the past.

Chapter Eight

COOP AND HIS dad stood on the sidewalk as the Bluebonnet Parade made its way down Main Street. Warm spring air and a cloudless sky made for a perfect day in Last Stand. If Coop had his way though, it'd be ten degrees cooler, but he wasn't complaining. No, not when Cassie was so excited about the festival.

"Look, there she is," his dad pointed out ten minutes into the parade.

Cassie was in line with the other children. Her kindness display was one of seven chosen from Mrs. Marquez's second grade classroom that best depicted the theme, and the children had taped their posters together to make one large banner. The children beamed, their smiles bright, but no one beamed as long or as hard as Cassie. And as soon as she spotted them, she lifted her hand to wave. They waved back, Coop so proud of his daughter for her accomplishments.

"That girl's poster kicked butt," his dad said, unabashed pride in his tone.

"I wonder why?"

"What? You think those other kids didn't have help from

their folks?"

Coop pursed his lips, keeping his mouth shut. He knew better than to get between Grandpa Joe and his granddaughter. Cassie's poster was all about her friendship with Taylor. His dad had encouraged her to draw out the scene and label it, "Kindness is when friends make you feel better when you are sad." It was picture of a small figure of Cassie and a grown-up figure of Taylor holding hands and wearing their heart-shaped necklaces with big smiles on their faces.

Coop took his eyes off Cassie just long enough to see Taylor watching along, standing beside Julie and Miguel on the sidewalk. Their eyes connected for a split second and in that flash, he was taken back to holding her in his arms and kissing her. The kiss that shouldn't have happened. The one that had kept him up half the night. He was beginning to fall for Taylor again and that just couldn't be. Raw pain gnawed at him. He was doing his very best with Cassie, but he didn't deserve another chance at love. Underlying guilt surfaced and the heartbreak of losing Francine still beat close to his heart. After he'd kissed Taylor, it had all come crashing down on him again. So, he'd minimized it in his head, pretended it meant nothing, and made sure Taylor didn't read too much into it. He'd driven her back to Julie's house, thanking her again for the dress, for her help with Cassie, and making sure Taylor understood the date was really one big thank-you. And then he'd rushed off, leaving her alone on the doorstep.

How unfair of him.

Cassie's class moved on, heading toward the park in the center of town and after the Creekbend High School marching band and the Last Stand Fire Department Engine 105 followed behind with hand-waving firefighters atop the shining apple red truck, the parade ended. All the spectators remaining on the streets headed to the park, where the Bluebonnet Festival was just beginning.

"THIS IS GREAT," Taylor said to Julie and Miguel. "All these years I've heard about the festival and now I'm getting to experience it myself." Around her, open air tents and makeshift booths lined the entire perimeter of the park. Balloons flew, banners waved and children ran by with wide-eyed joy in their eyes. Smoke billowed up at one corner of the park where barbeques were set up, cooking burgers and dogs, chicken and brisket. Fried foods were offered in abundance. Some booths housed games where adults and children alike could win prizes. Every kind of dessert was represented—rainbow snow cones, blue cotton candy, funnel cakes and five flavors of ice cream.

This was the most people she'd ever seen congregate in town. Had the entire population of Last Stand come out for the festival?

"It's a lot of fun," Julie said. "I'm glad you're here."

"Me too," Miguel said. "Small-town life has a way of creeping up on you."

"Why do I get the feeling you're trying to tell me something?"

Miguel smiled wide. "Just stating a fact, Taye."

"You two are so darn calm. Next week at this time, you'll be saying your vows. And look at you, neither one of you have a care in the world."

"That's because we have you to worry for us," Miguel teased.

"Seriously, you've been such a big help to us that it's made it easy," Julie added.

Taylor was just about to comment when Julie and Miguel glanced over her shoulder. She swiveled around and found Blake Charles approaching, a smile on his face.

"Hello, Taylor. Julie, Miguel."

They greeted him politely and as Blake was shaking Miguel's hand, Julie sent her a questioning look, her brows gathered.

"Enjoying your first Bluebonnet Festival, Taylor?" Blake asked.

He wore a button-down blue shirt open at the collar and dark slacks. He looked every bit the businessman, even in this casual setting. He was tall and nice-looking and any shyness he'd had years ago had washed clean away through time.

"I am. This is such a wonderful display of community."

"It is. We have a booth over there." He pointed toward his Charles Realty sign across the way. "We're sponsoring a game this year. Ring toss. Lots of good prizes for the kids. Be sure to come on by."

"We definitely will," Julie said.

Taylor found the booth and nodded. "Yes, I'll give it a try too." But just as she was turning away, her gaze landed on Coop.

He stood next to Cassie and Grandpa Joe in line at the cotton candy booth. He eyed her and then shifted to Blake, who was standing directly next to her. Coop's mouth became a rigid line of disapproval. Every nerve in Taylor's body pinched tight. She didn't need Coop's approval to speak with a friend. The man couldn't have it both ways.

"I wonder if I could steal you away for a few minutes?" Blake was asking.

"What?" She gave him her attention. "I'm sorry," she said to him, shaking her head.

"I have a few questions for you and thought we could take a minute to talk?"

She glanced at Coop again and then nodded sweetly. "Of course, I'd love to speak with you. Why don't we take a little walk? Julie, Miguel, I'll meet up with you a little later, okay?"

"Sure," Julie said.

"See you in a few," Miguel offered.

And when Blake smiled at her, she smiled back, sensing Coop's eyes were shooting flaming arrows at her back.

Blake bought her a waffle ice cream cone, strawberry with sprinkles on top, and they moved through the festival, looking at the booths. She tried her hand at ring toss at his realty booth with Blake cheering her on. They moved on, both enjoying their cones, but the noise was a bit much, so when Blake suggested they stroll down the street, she immediately agreed.

"Did you have questions about your sister's wedding gown?" she asked, a bit curious about why he'd sought her out in the first place.

"I do, but I also wanted to spend a little time with you. If you don't mind."

"I, uh, oh, that's nice." And it was. He was a good distraction from Coop. Just thinking about him and his sour puss, annoyed her no end. "Of course I don't mind." She licked her cone, the strawberry sliding down her throat easily. The combination of strawberry and chocolate sprinkles, too good to be legal. "This is so yummy."

Blake took a bite from of his plain vanilla cone. Somehow, she knew he'd be a vanilla kind of guy. But she wasn't judging him. He was nice and had kind brown eyes. Finally, he got to asking about the wedding gown, but she got the feeling he was just making questions up. At least he was forthcoming and honest about wanting to spend time with her.

Unlike a certain cowboy contractor she knew.

They found themselves on the corner of Bluebonnet and

Laurel, several blocks from the park. It was quieter now, the buzz of festivities a tiny hum in her ears. They stopped, waiting for traffic, and Taylor saw her reflection in the glass window, then realized she was looking into an empty space that used to be The Purple Pansy. "What happened to Jo Beth's dress shop?"

"Jo Beth's husband retired and they decided to move closer to her daughter in Arizona. She closed up shop about two months ago."

"Really?"

He gave her a solemn nod. "Jo Beth had mixed feelings about leaving. She loved her shop. Had a big close-out sale and practically everything sold. Now the place is for sale."

"Oh, well…good for her. It must've been a tough decision. She always seemed to enjoy her shop. Sometimes, Julie and I would wander in here and browse around. Her clothes were distinct. She had good taste."

"So do you," Blake said. "My sister is quite taken with your designs. I think she'll be calling you soon about one of the gowns. How long are you planning on staying in Last Stand?"

"I'm supposed to leave right after Julie's wedding."

"That soon?" Blake seemed disappointed.

"But anytime Connie wants to speak to me, I'll be available to her."

"Thanks, I appreciate that. I'll let her know."

"Maybe we should head back to the festival now?" She'd

eaten her last bite of ice cream, gobbling up the very bottom tip of the waffle cone, her favorite part.

Once they reached the park, she thanked Blake again for the ice cream. "I should probably get back to Miguel and Julie."

"Sure, okay. Thanks for the walk. Uh, I guess I'll be talking to you," he said, lingering awkwardly as if he wanted to say more.

She wasn't sure she wanted to hear what he had to say. "Bye, Blake, thanks again."

She took off toward the Friends of the Library booth and then spotted Miguel and Julie at the Outlaw Tequila photo booth speaking with Coop and his dad. Deep in conversation, they didn't notice her, so she spun around and was making a quick getaway when Cassie's voice stopped her in her tracks. "Taylor, look at me! I'm *in* the wanted poster!"

Taylor turned and sure enough, Cassie was posing in a cutout wanted poster, twin gun barrels crossing overhead, labeling her WANTED for $1,000. She was all smiles as the photographer clicked away, taking her photo.

Taylor walked over and greeted them.

"Where'd you go before?" Cassie asked innocently, shuffling away from the cutout. "I've been looking for you."

"You've been looking for me?" Taylor bent to her level. "Well, I saw you in the parade, Cassie, and your poster really stood out. I'm proud of your hard work. Tell me, was it fun being in the parade?"

"It was kinda cool. I'm glad you liked the poster. Grandpa helped me with it, but I wrote all the words and did all the coloring."

"You did a great job, Cassie. And, hey, I like the dress you're wearing." It was a denim overall dress with a bib and straps, and a white T-shirt underneath. Her hair was separated in two perfect braids, blond bangs coming loose on her forehead. Even if it wasn't exactly the most feminine outfit, it was progress and Cassie looked adorable. Taylor tugged on the denim strap and grinned.

"Daddy took me shopping."

"You look very pretty."

"Thanks."

Taylor stood and smiled at Grandpa Joe and Miguel, keeping her distance from Coop. She didn't much like how he judged her being with Blake. It was uncalled for.

Cassie slipped her small hand in hers. "Daddy, can Taylor take a picture with us? You said we could take one more picture in the wanted booth."

Oh, boy, she didn't want to disappoint the child, but she didn't belong in a family photo. That was for darn sure. "Oh, well…I don't know. Why don't you take one with your dad and grandpa?"

"And you, Taylor. Pleeeze."

Her sweet, pleading voice traveled straight to Taylor's heart.

"The three of you go on," Grandpa Joe said. "I've had

enough pictures for one day. Go on, Taylor. Coop. Don't want to let Cassie down now."

Coop shot his dad a hard look that said he didn't like his manipulating. Taylor wasn't thrilled with it either, but Cassie was tugging her hand toward the cutout. And Coop went along with it, presumably not to disappoint his daughter.

"You sure?" he asked softly enough for only her to hear. "Being as it's a wanted photo, I'm surprised Blake hasn't dragged you over here with him."

The smugness of his tone cut deep and she lashed out. "How do you know he didn't?"

Disbelief stole over his face, as if she'd gotten him good, but then he shrugged. "Nah, ice cream's more his style."

How did he know that? "Seems you've been spying on me."

"Get real, Taylor. Cassie spotted you licking at your…waffle cone."

"Sometimes, Coop, you're a real jerk," she whispered.

"You like him?"

"None of your beeswax."

"That's real grown-up of you."

"You're jealous."

"Am not."

"Then why'd you bring it up?"

"Would you two stop bickering like an old married couple and take the darn photo already? Cassie is waiting," Julie said.

Indeed, Cassie had dropped her hand and run up to the sign, impatiently waiting for them to pose for the picture.

It wasn't the first time Julie had to break up an argument between the two of them. One time, it got so bad, Julie pulled out a coach's whistle and blew it so long and so loud, the neighbors complained. Her friendship with Coop had spanned both extremes, love and hate, and right now she was edging toward the negative.

Taylor plastered on a smile she didn't feel for Cassie's sake, rubbing shoulders with Coop as he fitted Cassie in front of them. All three crowded into the cutout, smiling to the camera as the photographer snapped several photos.

When they were through, Cassie turned, arms wide, and gave them both a big hug. It was sweet, nothing about Cassie wasn't, but Taylor's eyes had nowhere else to go but to sink deep into Coop's baby blues and get lost there.

Her stomach tied up in knots, aching like the devil, and she moved away from him.

"Something wrong, Taylor?" Grandpa Joe asked, his gray brows furrowing. "You're looking pale all of a sudden."

She put a hand to her stomach. "I think I ate too much."

"Those waffle cones will do that to you every time," Coop stated.

She gave him a look. They were no longer speaking about ice cream and she mentally sighed.

He cared about her, she knew that much, but she had to

tough it out, and not give in to the feelings she had for him. Or acknowledge the feelings he had for her. He *had* been jealous, even if he wouldn't admit it. But he also wasn't ready...for anything. And she knew that too.

She lifted her head. "You know what, I'm not going to let a little tummy ache stop me from enjoying the rest of the festival. I think I'm going to try my hand at balloon darts. Miguel, I hear you're a ringer. Care to take me on?"

"Ah, sure, Taylor. But I have to warn you, I'm a pretty good aim."

"So am I, when I have the perfect target in mind." She glanced at Coop and once he caught on, his mouth hardened.

Enough said.

She walked off, feeling just a tad bit triumphant.

AFTER THE FESTIVAL, the days flew by with Julie and Miguel's wedding approaching fast. There was excitement in the air, the she-shed was almost done, and Taylor had put the finishing touches on Julie's gown. Taylor had gone to her second baseball game, something she'd promised Cassie, and it had been fun. The Tigers won the game, and Cassie had been ecstatic, asking her to join the team for pizza afterward. Taylor declined politely, making up a viable excuse.

She and Julie were in the midst of finalizing the catering

menu for Friday night's rehearsal dinner, which put pressure on Coop and his crew to have the she-shed painted and ready, since the dinner was to be held in the backyard. And Taylor's father was due here by Thursday. She was anxious to see him. He'd never been a part of their summers here, he spent every summer doing missionary work, so he didn't know Last Stand the way she did.

In a quiet moment on Wednesday evening, while Julie and Miguel were out shopping, Muffy snuggled up close to Taylor on the sofa, resting her blond head on her lap. Taylor gave her ear rubs and lots of hugs, petting her furry coat while Muffy attempted to lick Taylor's face.

"You're a good girl now, aren't you?" True, Muffy had calmed lately, making no escape attempts.

The pup had learned a valuable lesson—the grass wasn't always greener on the other side. And she'd learned it quicker than many mere humans had. Muffy was still rambunctious and overly affectionate, but she couldn't blame her for that. Everyone wanted love. And Taylor realized how much she would miss this little ball of fluff when she returned home. She squeezed Muffy tightly and kissed the very top of her head, between the ears. "You've been a good friend, Muff."

The doorbell rang, and Muffy hopped off her lap and raced to the front door, squeaking out a tiny bark too adorable to be any threat to the person behind the door.

Taylor scooped the pup in her arms and opened the door surprised to see Nicole there. "Hi!"

"Hi, Taylor. I hope I'm not catching you at a bad time."

"Not at all, I was just brainstorming with Muffy and we've determined that she likes belly rubs a bit more than ear rubs, but she wouldn't refuse either one."

Nicole laughed. "I think she's a wise little girl."

"Would you like to come in? Julie isn't here. The lovebirds are running errands right now."

"Actually, I came to see you." She ducked her head and blinked a few times.

Curious, she opened the door wider and stepped aside. "Then definitely come in. Things are quiet here at the moment." She led her to the parlor and they both sat on the sofa. "Would you like a cool drink?"

"No, thanks. I'm good."

"I can't believe the wedding is in a few days. All the preparation. We're finally coming down to the home stretch."

"I know. The time went by so quickly. Makes me think how fast my wedding is coming up. Which is…why I'm here. I really hate to ask you this…but Julie seemed to think it'd be all right. I don't want to impose, but I have a favor to ask."

Taylor figured it had something to do with her wedding gown. She was getting married in September. "You can ask me anything. If I can do something for you, let me know."

Obviously relieved, Nicole sighed. "Thanks. It's just that, I fell in love with one of your designs and I, well, I was hoping you'd be able to make my dress for me."

"Oh." Taylor blinked, confused. "I thought you had a dress all picked out, Nicole."

She shook her head. "It didn't compare to yours. And I have a special request. That is…if you're willing." She lifted hopeful eyes to her.

"What would that be?"

"I want my dress to be pale rose. In your design." Nicole blew out a breath.

"How about we see the design you're talking about." Taylor rose to grab her computer. She opened it and logged on, coming up with the folder holding her designs. "Which one do you like?"

"All of them," Nicole said, "but this one is me." She pointed to the third design in the layout, an off-the-shoulder gown and sweetheart neck with a side slit trumpet skirt and a scalloped train. The gown was perfect for Nicole's sleek shape. It showed flashes of skin, but with Nicole's lithe form, it would look great on her.

"That's called 'Chancy.' Yes, I can see this on you in pale rose. I think it would work nicely."

"You do?"

"It's a good choice for you."

"Do you think you could make it for me?"

"I, uh…I would love to, Nicole. But the logistics might prove difficult. I'm here only until after the wedding."

"I see." Disappointment rang in her voice. "I guess it's

too much to ask."

"You know when I made Julie's gown, I fitted it to myself, because we are basically the same size. But with you, all I could do is take your measurements and hope for the best. And I couldn't promise you a good outcome."

"Of course. I just thought I'd ask." Her shoulders pulled down. "I really love that gown."

A ridiculous thought flashed in Taylor's mind. And why not? It wasn't as if she was running home to anything. Making Nicole's gown would bring her an income and would justify her staying just a little bit longer. "Unless..." she thought out loud. "I stay, just until I can finish your gown."

Nicole's eyes widened and she smiled. "Could you do that?"

"I mean, I think I could. If I can get the fabric I need in time, and if it's okay with Julie. They'd be on their honeymoon, so I could watch Muffy for them. It's a possibility."

"Oh, my goodness. That would be so great." Nicole reached over and hugged her tight, unable to contain her excitement. "Thank you so much."

"I can't promise you, it depends on a lot of things falling into place, but I'm going to try my hardest. That I *can* promise you."

"That's good enough for me."

And after she said goodbye to Nicole, she stood on the porch a long time, deep in thought and surprisingly, felt darn good about her decision.

ON THURSDAY EVENING, Miguel, Julie and her father, Zachary, welcomed Taylor's dad to their home with heartfelt hugs. "I'm so glad you're here, Uncle Jay," Julie said, hugging him tight. "I've missed you."

Her dad looked Julie up and down and shook his head. "It has been a while since we've seen each other. Julie, you're as lovely as ever."

"It's good to meet you, sir." Miguel stuck out his hand and the two men shook. "I'm glad you could make it."

"Same here," her dad said. "And where else would I be when my favorite niece is getting married?"

Everyone chuckled.

But then, her uncle Zachary looked at her dad and that quick glance acknowledged what they'd been thinking—their wives should be here too, to witness Julie's marriage. Both women died way too young and in that one moment the sweeping pain in their fathers' eyes, the resigned fall of their shoulders, the slight tight twist of their lips spoke of their great loss. Heartbreak was universal and, right now, it touched each and every one of them silently. The women had been great wives and mothers, and not to recognize them in this instant wouldn't have felt right. Julie and Taylor exchanged glances and knew that this moment was sacred, meant only for thoughts of their moms.

Taylor's dad was a strong man, steeped in faith and devotion, but when her mother died, it was as if his light had dimmed inside. Slowly, over time his light had begun to glow again and he was able to enjoy life. Taylor had grieved for her mom just as hard so she knew what he'd been going through. She was sure it was the same for Julie.

Muffy pawed at her dad's legs, begging for attention, and he bent to pick her up and give the fluff behind her ears a good scratching. The dog practically cooed. "You're a good girl, Muffy," her dad said. All eyes riveted to the dog and the solemn moment was broken.

"You think she's good? You should've seen me chasing her in Julie's wedding gown on my first day here. This girl," Taylor said, looking at Muffy and speaking in her baby voice, "will keep you on your toes if you're not careful."

"She's gotten better. Taylor's a good influence on her," Julie said.

"Taylor always is," her father said proudly. "But how on earth did you catch her in a wedding gown?"

"She had help," Julie explained. "Coop spotted a vision in white running down the street and couldn't believe his eyes when it was Taylor. He went after Muffy in his truck and then brought them both safely back. It was quite the homecoming."

And Coop's first words to her, stuck in Taylor's head. *What poor guy are you running away from this time?*

If she was running, she wasn't going fast enough to stop Coop's image from flashing in her head at odd times during the day. She wasn't going fast enough to halt her emotions from taking a wild and dangerous turn. And if she was running, then why was the thought of leaving Last Stand piercing her heart so badly?

"So, your friend Coop lives here again?" her dad asked, giving her a glance. Taylor nodded but said no more.

"He does. Matter of fact," her uncle Zachary said, "he's outside putting the finishing touches on Julie's wedding present. He and his crew have built her a she-shed."

"A she-shed," her dad repeated. "What a concept."

"It's going to be my reading room and library. Would you like to see it?" Julie asked. "That is, if you're not too tired from your trip, Uncle Jay."

"I'm fine, and would love to see it."

"Let's all go out and take a look, why don't we?" Miguel suggested.

The pack of them walked out the kitchen door. Coop turned his head away from the structure several yards away and found Taylor first, his stark blue eyes landing on hers. Wearing a tool belt over faded jeans, a white T-shirt stretched tight across his chest and his mountainous biceps exposed, Taylor's breath hitched in her throat. His eyes alone, when piercing hers, was enough to make her dizzy. The rest was just a bonus.

She put her head down as the group walked over to the

shed, yet she sensed his gaze on her still.

"Taylor!" Cassie's voice broke the moment, thankfully, and she came running over, all smiles.

She wrapped her arms around Taylor's waist and hugged tight. Taylor's heart melted just a little bit more.

"Hi, Cass. Working with your daddy again?"

"Yep. I have enough to buy my new mitt now."

"That's wonderful. I'm proud of you for sticking with it." She tugged on Cassie's braid. "Hey, would you like to meet my dad?"

Cassie bobbed her head up and down. Taylor spun Cass around to face her father.

"Dad, this is Cassie. She's Ryan Cooper's daughter. Cassie's going to be the flower girl in the wedding."

"You don't say? Well, nice to meet you, Cassie." Her father lifted his palm and Cassie high-fived him. Her dad was perceptive and knew the minute he laid eyes on Cass she was a high-fiver and not a hand-shaker.

Coop walked over and immediately put out his hand. "Nice to finally meet you, sir. I'm Ryan, but everyone around here calls me Coop."

"Well, yes. Hello, Coop. I'm Jay. Glad to meet you. Of course, I've heard about you from Taylor. After she'd return from Last Stand, she'd have story after story to tell. Seems to me, you three had some wonderful summers together."

Coop gave Julie a glance, then looked at her with a wide smile. "Yes, we did. That's for sure."

"Daddy is coach on my Tigers baseball team," Cassie piped up.

"Well, isn't that just fine. Seems your daddy has many talents." Her dad looked over at the she-shed. "I hear you've finished up on the she-shed."

"Isn't it great?" Julie gushed. "Coop did an amazing job."

"Thanks. It's just about finished on the inside. You can pop your head in, but the paint isn't quite dry so be careful."

All of them took turns peeking in. Taylor loved the interior, with light wood and white bookshelves lining two walls, a counter space for her computer and plenty of room for seating. The exterior was equally impressive with a porch and sitting area, double glass door entryway and cottage-type windows that welcomed light.

Everyone sang his praises and rightfully so. Taylor loved what he'd created for Julie.

"It's just perfect," Julie said, rising up on tiptoes to kiss Coop on the cheek. "Thank you."

"Hey, where's mine?" Miguel gave her a crooked smile. "It was my idea."

"And it's a wonderful gift. Even if the two of you conspired behind my back to surprise me." She gave her fiancé a kiss on the cheek too. "You're both the best. Hey, why don't you and Cassie stay for dinner?" she said to Coop. "We'd love to have you and there's plenty of food. Your dad is welcome too."

Taylor snapped her eyes to Julie. Of course, Julie could

invite anyone she wanted to her house for dinner, but Taylor had been trying her best to steer clear of Coop. And she had for the better part of the week. She'd been on her computer searching for fabric and driving to neighboring towns, gathering the right material and sequins and lace for Nicole's wedding gown. The project gave her something else to think about and she was anxious to get started. Julie had been thrilled that Taylor was going to stay on for two more weeks, and well, maybe her cousin had been hoping part of that reason was because of Coop. But it wasn't. Not really. It was about figuring out her future and needing more time.

Coop eyed her and she couldn't quite hide the deep frown on her face that said *no. Don't join us.* She was being selfish, or maybe just clinging to survival, but it was getting too darn hard to be around him.

"Thanks for the invite, but we can't. Cassie and I have plans tonight."

"Daddy! Why can't we stay? I really, really want to."

"I know, Cass." His voice soft, he added, "We have that school project to finish. If you want my help, it has to be tonight."

"But, Daddy." Cassie gave Taylor a pleading look that said *help me*. It made her heart hurt to see the little girl's disappointment. But she couldn't help. She couldn't go against Coop's decision even though she was fairly sure she'd played a part in him declining the invitation.

"I said no, Cassie. Sorry. Thanks again, Julie. But we're

gonna have to pass this time. You folks have a nice dinner."

Cassie had a pout on her face, her lower lip quivering as she walked out the door with her daddy.

Taylor felt like a heel and after they left, she excused herself and went to her room, plopping down on the bed. She just needed a minute alone to gather her thoughts. But it wasn't her thoughts that were bothering her. It was her feelings, coming from deep inside that unsettled her, making her rethink her every decision.

A knock at the door startled her and she sat up straighter.

"It's me, Taylor," her dad said.

"Oh, Dad, come in."

He walked into the room and sat down next to her on the bed. "Hi."

"Hi." His presence was always so calming. He had a way of making people feel included and loved. She was always so proud of the work he was doing, the ministry that he helped.

"How's my little girl?"

"I'm fine, Dad."

He gave his head a shake and a wisp of thick gray hair fell onto his forehead. "I know that you're not."

"Don't I look happy?" She plastered on a smile.

"To others maybe, but not to me." He took her hand, entwining their fingers. "What's wrong, Taylor?"

"Besides the fact that I don't have a job?"

"Yes, besides that. That little Cassie is awfully cute. And her father couldn't peel his eyes away from you."

"Cassie is a doll, and Coop, well, he's just a friend."

"Seems to me, it's more than that. You two have been friends a long time. You've had a history since childhood. I can see that something's there between you."

"Maybe, I don't know. There's so many things in the way. He's a widower, and very cautious about letting go. He lives here. I live on the East Coast. Right now, I'm jobless. And, well, I made Mom a promise I'd pursue my dreams and be successful. And that's what I'm trying to do."

"Sometimes in life, dreams change, honey. Don't hold yourself to a higher standard than anyone else. I don't have any answers for you. But I will ask you to do one thing and that's to be honest with yourself. Be true to the woman you are today. Usually, when you do that, things fall into place."

"Thanks, Dad. I will."

"Promise?"

He knew what he was asking. This was a hard one to promise. Being honest with herself could mean heartbreak and she might have to face another kind of rejection. But her father was right. She needed to face the truth about herself and her dreams and what she really wanted out of life.

"I promise."

He gave her hand a squeeze and then placed a kiss to her cheek.

"Dad?"

"Hmm?"

"I'm glad you're here."

"So am I, honey."

THE WEDDING REHEARSAL went off without a hitch, and after going through a dry run at the church, the wedding party all returned to Julie's house for dinner. Well, except for Cassie and her dad. They'd come to the rehearsal, Cassie doing her part very well, pretending to toss rose petals along the aisle and taking her place next to the bridesmaids up at the altar, but afterward, Coop had taken Cassie home. He'd told Julie Grandpa Joe wasn't feeling well and Coop didn't want to leave him alone for too long. Besides, it was going to be a long day for Cassie tomorrow. There was no arguing with those reasons.

At the house, Taylor took over, giving Julie and Miguel a break from any worries about the dinner. It was their time to shine. Taylor dealt with the caterers, the table rentals and background music. After a lovely three-course meal of sweet kale salad, walnut chicken divan, roasted baby potatoes and yeast rolls, the bride-to-be stood up and gave a toast. "To my dear family and friends, I'm so glad all of you are here to share this special time with Miguel and me. We are humbled and love you all very much. To my father, Zachary, for your love and generosity and for always being there when I needed you. You are the best father in the world. I love you, Dad."

Taylor's eyes burned with tears ready to be shed. Tears

she tried to hold back.

"And to my wonderful uncle Jay, for making the trip to Last Stand to officiate our wedding. Having you marry us means more than you could possibly know."

A sole tear dripped down Taylor's cheek. She was a sucker for sentiment.

"To my bridesmaids, Nicole and Lindsey, your friendship has meant so much to me. I want to thank you from the bottom of my heart for being in my wedding. You guys know I love you." Julie put her head down, sighed and then stared straight at Taylor. "And, lastly, before I turn this over to Miguel, I want to thank my cousin Taylor for being here with me for my special day. She came all the way from New York to help me with our wedding. Our summers together here in Last Stand were special times and as little girls, we'd often daydream about the day we'd marry, planning the day down to very specific details and fantasizing about our dream dress. Well, my dear, talented cousin, you've made my dream come true. You've designed the most beautiful wedding gown for me, and you've helped me so much over these past few weeks. I'll never forget it. You are truly one of a kind, cousin, and I'm thankful every day I have you in my life."

Taylor smiled at Julie, her cousin's sweet words hitting her heart with enough emotion to open the floodgates. Tears streamed down her face, streaking her makeup as they dripped onto the floor. Her shoulders slightly shook. She couldn't help it. She was mush inside right now and filled with an abundance of love for her family. For Julie most of all. Her cousin who was really a sister to her.

Words wouldn't come. They weren't necessary. She blew Julie a kiss and knew her cousin would understand all that kiss meant.

After all the toasts were done, Julie handed out gifts to her wedding party. The girls all received a pair of rose-toned earrings to wear tomorrow for the wedding and the guys received a monogrammed beer stein. Apparently, it was some sort of private joke between Miguel, his two brothers and his father, who was his best man. The entire male half of the Herrera family was in the wedding. It was the way Miguel wanted it. He and his dad had had a rocky road in the past, and according to Julie, having him as best man signified their late, but close bond.

By the end of the evening, after all the guests were gone and Taylor was cleaning up the last remnants of the dinner, dealing with the caterers and straightening up the house, she received a text message from Coop. Alarmed, her initial thought was of Grandpa Joe. Why else would Coop be contacting her at this late hour? But she was wrong. Coop's text wasn't about that. He wanted to see her. Tonight. If she wasn't too tired.

Too darn curious not to agree, she texted him back right away and waited for him under the dim light illuminating the front porch steps. It was almost midnight and she wondered what couldn't wait until the morning.

His truck pulled up quietly and he parked alongside the curb under a birch tree. He emerged out of the shadows carrying a rectangular gift box and sat down beside her. He set the box on the porch. "Hi," he said softly.

"Hi. Is everything all right? Is your dad..."

"He's fine. He was tired and feeling a bit weak, but he's sleeping now. I think he's got a bug of some sort."

"That's good to hear. I mean, not that he's sick but—"

"I know what you mean. He's getting up there in age and he's just realizing he's got to slow down a bit. No more running 5K marathons."

"Or dancing 'til dawn," she added, smiling.

"Or speed racing."

"Or skinny dipping at midnight."

Coop made a face. "Perish the thought."

They laughed and Coop got comfortable, stretching his long legs out on the steps.

Taylor sighed, looking out at the few stars in the dark sky. Coop too simply stared straight ahead. It was easy, the two of them sitting here together, saying nothing, just being.

Like old times.

"Can't believe Julie's big day is tomorrow," she said finally.

"Yeah."

Coop seemed in no hurry to tell her what this was all about. Had he simply wanted to drop off a present for Julie and Miguel?

They sat another minute quietly. It was weird, though the air seemed charged around them, they were both at peace. As if trying to avoid each other these past days had disappeared and they were simply allowing themselves a moment of reprieve.

Taylor opened her mouth, unable to hold back the yawn that forced its way through her lips. It wasn't the company, but she'd had a long day and her body was calling it quits.

Coop let out a big sigh, then grabbed the gift from the porch. "I thought there'd be a lot going on tomorrow with the wedding and all, so here, Taylor. This is for you," he said softly, setting the gift on her lap.

"For me? What? Why?" She was baffled, not expecting the gift to be for her.

"Just open it. You'll see."

She opened the pretty box and unfolded the paper inside to reveal a collage picture frame. "Oh, Coop."

"Do you know what it is?"

Tears pooled in her eyes and she nodded, too choked up to speak.

"It's made from remnants of the gazebo. After we tore it down, I saved some of the better wood."

"So I'll always have a piece of the gazebo with me. This is…" She couldn't put her sentiments to words right now. It was the most thoughtful gift she'd ever received.

"I know how much the gazebo meant to you and Julie. Hers is hanging up in the she-shed as a surprise."

"Thank...you." She was moved, touched by his kindness. Touched he'd given one to her and Julie as well. It meant that much more. Taylor's emotions ran up and down like an out of whack elevator. Theirs was a complicated relationship, but this was...so unexpected.

"I...love...it, Coop. Really. Where did you get these pictures?" There were seven photos in all ranging from when they were six until their teen years. Beautiful pictures of Aunt Suzie and her mom. Of her and Coop alone, of the Three Musketeers, swimming, playing, having fun. Memories that would remain with her always.

"Miguel did some snooping for me. That's all I'm gonna say."

She looked into his eyes, saw them gleaming, proud of his work, but also happy he'd surprised her. And right then she knew she was in love with Ryan Cooper. Wholly. Fully. Completely.

She'd tried not to be. Tried to avoid him and protect her heart, but none of that had worked. How could she not love a man who was a good father and son, a man who was as infuriating as he was kind, a man who'd been hurt too much in life not to shy away from love again? How could she not love her childhood friend, her teenage sweetheart? The guy who'd been a constant in her life, even when she didn't realize it?

"You and Miguel do a lot of conspiring, don't you?"

He said nothing, simply stared at the joy in her eyes.

She hugged the frame to her chest. "It's a pretty great midnight gift, Coop."

"Is it that late?" he asked softly.

She nodded.

"Maybe I should've waited until tomorrow, but I wanted to give it to you before you left for New York."

She blinked. "Oh, I guess you don't know. I'm not leaving."

His head snapped back. "You're not?"

"No, not for a while anyway. I have contracted work here."

"When did all this happen?" He seemed confused.

"Just a few days ago. I'll be staying while Julie and Miguel are on their honeymoon. Watching Muffy and working."

He nodded and smiled. "Okay."

Okay? What did that mean? Was he happy or disappointed? Or was he already plotting ways to avoid her again?

"I'd better let you get some sleep." Coop rose then and gave her a hand to help her up. Their faces inches apart, they stared at each other for a moment and then Taylor rose up on tiptoes and gave him a kiss on the cheek.

"Thanks again, Coop. It's the best gift I've ever received."

He nodded and walked away. She saw him smiling until he was swallowed up by the shadows.

Five minutes later, after stashing Coop's gift in the closet, hidden behind her clothes so Julie wouldn't find it, she heard

Muffy scratching at Julie's door.

Taylor took a peek and found Julie opening the door for the dog. "Time for bed, Muff," she said.

"Julie?" she whispered. "You're not asleep yet?"

"No, too much excitement, I guess."

"Can we talk? Just for a minute?"

"Sure. Come in."

The girls sat down on Julie's bed.

"It's late and I won't take but a minute. But I promised you something and now I'm keeping that promise," Taylor said.

"Gosh, what promise? You've already done so much for me."

"Remember I said you'd be the first to know when I know about my feelings for Coop?"

"Are you telling me now you know for sure?"

She nodded. "I love him, Jules. So much."

Julie took both of her hands and squeezed until the blood stopped flowing. "I knew it!"

"I'm scared, Julie. Really, really scared."

"Don't be. Enjoy the feeling. Revel in it. Love is an amazing thing and I'm happy you finally figured it out."

"Did I?"

"You will, honey. I know it'll all work out. Now, it's time for our beauty sleep. We both have a big day tomorrow."

"Yes, and I can't wait. Good night, Jules."

"Night, my maid of honor extraordinaire."

Chapter Nine

THE NEXT AFTERNOON, Taylor opened the door to Coop and Cassie. Coop was in his work clothes, Cassie in her jeans. "I think this young lady needs some assistance getting ready for the wedding," Coop said. "Seems someone promised to do her hair."

Taylor grinned. "That would be me. Hi, Cassie. Are you ready?"

Cassie put her head down. "I guess so."

Taylor gazed into Coop's deep blue eyes, her heart as full as it's ever been. She wondered if he could see a difference in her, in the way she was looking at him. Was the evidence of her love written all over her face?

Coop winked as if to say Cassie would be all right. And then Taylor knew he hadn't picked up on her newfound emotions. His concern was for his daughter. As it should be.

"Did you bring your special necklace?" she asked.

"Sure did." He took a jewelry box out of his pocket and slipped it into his daughter's hand. "Here you go, Cassie. I know you'll take good care with it."

"I will, Daddy."

Cassie met Taylor's eyes. "You're going to wear yours, right?"

"I sure am." Taylor put out her hand. "Ready? I've got an idea of what to do with your hair. I think you're gonna like it."

She looked at her dad and when he nodded, she took Taylor's hand. "Go on, Cass. You're gonna do fine, honey. Just like you did at rehearsal yesterday." He bent to kiss Cassie's cheek. "Dad's gotta get ready for the wedding too. Grandpa and I will see you both at the church a little later, okay?"

Taylor put her hands over Cassie's shoulders. "Don't worry about a thing. Us girls, we'll be just fine."

Cassie finally cracked a smile and Coop gave them both one last look before he left.

"We have a couple of hours, Cass. The other girls are getting their hair and makeup done right now downstairs. Let's start on your hair. And then we'll both get dressed. How's that?"

"Okay," Cassie said, her mood brightening a bit.

They entered the house and she took Cassie upstairs where Taylor set out all her grooming paraphernalia. Hair straighteners, blowers, curling irons, combs and brushes took up most of the counter space.

She began brushing Cassie's hair. "I love your long hair, Cass. I think we should leave it down in the back. You don't mind if I do your hair like mine, do you? Here, I'll show you."

Taylor parted her hair down the middle in the front and began braiding Cassie's hair on each side. Then she connected the braids in the back to make one longer braid, all the while leaving the rest of her hair to fall softly down her back. It took a few tries to get the hairdo just right, but when she was done, she handed Cassie a mirror to look at it from all sides. "What do you think?"

She smiled. "It's just like yours."

"Yep, that was the plan. And we all have a little tiara of fresh flowers to go in our hair. Here we go," she said, placing the headband of baby roses onto her head. "It's just right, Cassie. You look very pretty."

Cassie was quiet, but she kept glancing at herself in the bathroom mirror, and with each glance, her acceptance seemed to grow.

"Time to put your dress on. You haven't been feasting on big ole chocolate bars every day, have you?"

Cassie chuckled. "No."

"Okay, so the dress should fit you just right."

Taylor took the dress off the hanger in her bedroom and handed it to Cassie. "Need some help with this?"

Cassie shook her head. 'I've got it."

Taylor stepped away for a few minutes to put on her own maid of honor dress. When she returned to Cassie, she found her wearing the flower girl dress and looking like a princess. She didn't make mention of that though. She had to tiptoe around her compliments, so Cassie wouldn't feel self-conscious.

Before she could say anything at all, Cassie turned to her. "You look pretty, Taylor."

"Oh, sweetheart, so do you, but wait a minute, we did forget something."

Taylor opened the jewelry box sitting on the counter and found a stunning ruby and diamond necklace there. She handled it with care and walked over to Cassie. "Here, Cass. Let's put this on you."

Cassie began to smile, a little bit nervously, and after Taylor latched the clasp, they both stared at the necklace through the mirror. "Cassie, this is very special. I love it on you."

"Me too." She fingered the piece carefully. "Daddy said my mommy would think I'm a big enough girl to wear this."

"Oh, Cass, I think so too." She placed her hands on Cassie's shoulders and gave a gentle squeeze. She whispered in her ear, "Super flower girl powers."

Cassie grinned and nodded.

Then Taylor retrieved her mother's necklace and fastened it around her neck. "There, now we're both ready for the wedding. Shall we go check on Julie? She might need our help."

Cassie took Taylor's hand and they walked downstairs to see how the bride-to-be was faring.

AT THE CHURCH, Taylor kissed her uncle Zachary and turned to give Julie a gentle hug before the procession began. "Be happy, Jules," she whispered. "I'm so excited for you."

"I'm excited too," Julie bubbled. Was there ever a more thrilled bride?

Then Taylor took her place.

When the music began to play, Lindsey started down the aisle and, after several beats, Nicole made her walk too, each bridesmaid taking measured steps. Taylor came next and she sighed. This was it. Julie was getting married and the time had come to make that maid of honor trip down the aisle. She did so as gracefully as she could, smiling and glancing at the guests in attendance. Miguel, his brothers and father were waiting patiently in the front. As Taylor reached the altar she stared into her father's light green eyes. Looking very reserved up there, staunch and ready to marry his niece, her father gave her a playful wink. Taylor grinned and then turned toward Cassie, who was ready to make her walk. She took her job as flower girl very seriously. When their eyes met, Taylor fingered her heart necklace and Cassie reached up to do the same. It was a special moment between the two of them, like they had a secret no one else knew about. Which indeed, was true. Then Cassie started down the aisle, her head held high, her steps careful as she tossed multicolored flower petals onto the white aisleway.

That-a-girl, Cassie.

Taylor took her eyes off Cassie just long enough to find Coop seated in the second row. Dressed in a black tailored suit, his shaggy dark hair groomed and making a slight flip at the neck, he looked devastatingly handsome. Her breath caught in her throat, but it wasn't his appearance that stole her breath, it was the deep, dark look of pride in his eyes, watching Cassie make her way down the aisle. The unabashed love he had for his daughter was evident on his face. Taylor found that father/daughter bond incredibly appealing. And for a moment, she ached to be included in that bond. But she refocused on the ceremony because once Cassie made it up the aisle and took her place with the bridesmaids, it was Julie's turn.

The first bars of the wedding march rang out and announced the appearance of the bride. Everyone rose from their seats and turned to face the back of the church. Julie was magnificent in ivory and lace and her mother's pearls. Oohs and ahhs were breathed out as she began her walk down the aisle. Happy tears formed in Julie's eyes, and that was all Taylor had to see. She wept silently, joyously, and took a quick second to brush her tears away with her index finger. Her heart was full, seeing Julie so happy. Miguel joined her at the altar, shaking hands with her uncle Zachary and then clasping Julie's hands in his.

Taylor's dad spoke eloquently about love and marriage, and Taylor let his words sink in. She'd been focused on her career and hadn't allowed anything to interfere, like a love life, but now as the ceremony was taking place, she realized what she wanted. What meant most to her.

And if her father's speech wasn't enough, the vows Miguel and Julie spoke to each other completed the ceremony and two had become one right before her eyes.

THE RECEPTION WAS held at The Arbors of Draeger Ranch, an event venue in the midst of peach orchards, lending a breathtaking natural backdrop. Tables and chairs were set up, along with fine white linens and stunning hydrangea arrangements were placed as centerpieces. Caterers were busy making dinner for seventy-five guests and a DJ was supplying predinner music on an outdoor dance floor.

"Dad, the ceremony was beautiful. You put your words together with such grace and humility."

"Thank you, Taylor. I wanted this one to be very special."

"It was."

"And speaking of special, Julie wore your wedding gown to perfection. I didn't miss the gasps from the wedding guests when Julie first appeared. You are very talented, Taylor. It's nothing new, but seeing Julie in something you designed is the icing on the cake."

Rarely did Taylor get the chance to see her designs in

action during the actual wedding, so her dad was right, this one was super special. Because it was Julie and also because Taylor could witness the bride in one of her designs in real time.

"Thank you. I'm pretty happy about how it turned out. I'm sort of a perfectionist."

"And it shows, honey."

A short time later, dinner was called. Taylor sat at the head table along with the rest of the wedding party, being paired up with Mr. Alberto Herrera. She and Miguel's father made light conversation during the meal and afterward it was time to dance.

The DJ didn't hold back, his playlist designed in part by Miguel and his heavy metal tendencies. When a more gentile song played, obviously Julie's choice in music, Alberto asked Taylor to dance. He took her hand as they made their way to the dance floor and together they moved to the soft rock tune. He was light on his feet and a wonderful partner.

Soon the dance floor filled up, Julie and Miguel taking center stage. It was fun being on the floor with them, seeing the joy in their eyes, seeing them cut loose.

Her feet aching, she finally took a seat after three dances with Alberto. As she glanced around, she didn't have to look hard to find Coop sitting at the table with Cassie. He'd danced with his daughter a few times, but in between he'd been bombarded with women, young and old, asking him to dance. He'd converse with them for a little bit, but he'd never once accepted their offer. The handsome widower attracted women like bees to honey. She'd love to say it didn't bother her, but who was she kidding? If she were a cat, her claws would be out. Although, Grandpa Joe didn't have a hard time accepting dance offers. He'd been on the dance floor quite a bit tonight.

Miguel walked over and asked her to dance. "The groom would like a dance with the MOH."

Taylor chuckled. "You've got the jargon down, don't you?'

He smiled. "I'm trying."

When he put out his hand, she was happy to take it and soon she was being whisked around the dance floor. "It's an amazing night," she said to him. "Is it everything you'd hoped it would be?"

"As long as Julie's happy, I'm happy. But yes, we're having a good time."

"You know what they say, Miguel. Happy wife, happy life."

"I have learned that valuable lesson."

"Then Julie's a very lucky girl."

"I won't disagree."

Just then, Taylor felt a tap on the back. She turned to find Cassie there. The little girl smiled wide, her eyes twinkling. "I'd like to cut in. For a dance with Miguel please."

Coop stood directly behind his daughter and when their eyes met, Coop gave her a helpless look. Cassie sure was a sly one. "Sure, you can cut in. Miguel, I bet you'd love a dance with this little flower girl."

"I certainly would," he said, taking Cassie's hands. "Let's do this."

The photographer was busy snapping photos, following Miguel's every movement, and when Taylor swiveled around, Coop was there offering his hand. "Want to dance?"

Sometimes in life, dreams change. Her father's wise words rang in her ear. She walked into Coop's arms, no longer cautious. She had an adventurous spirit and tonight she was going to let it fly. "I'd love to."

Coop held her tightly, his hand splayed over her back, keeping her close. She breathed in his scent, a combination of earth and man. It was so very appealing and familiar. She didn't want to scare him, or push him, but it was clear to her what she wanted in life now. And it wasn't a new job in New York. It wasn't to be renowned in her field. After seeing Julie in her gown today, she figured out what made her happiest was to bring her clients joy by designing a gown with all the personal touches that make it special for the bride.

"You're deep in thought," Coop said, staring at her.

She liked being the focus of his attention. "I'm just happy."

He pulled back. "You are? Did you get a job?"

"No, silly. I'm happy for Julie and Miguel. And all…brides."

"All brides?" His brows gathered, puzzled.

"Never mind. It's a girl thing. Cassie seems to be doing fine. She's having fun."

"Yeah, thanks to you. Whatever you two talked about brought her out of her shell."

"I'm glad."

"She's also pretty sly. Getting us to dance together."

"Well, you weren't making the first move." She batted her eyes at him and he chuckled.

"Miguel's dad had filled up your dance card."

"He is pretty light on his feet."

"And I'm a big oaf?"

"I didn't say that! You're doing just fine."

"Just fine?" Coop got a determined look in his eye and then clutched her tight and twirled her around the dance floor, his steps fluid and graceful and, well, she had no clue he could move like that.

Her head fell back as they swayed and turned to the rhythm, Taylor keeping step with him. It was exhilarating and thrilling, soulful beats living inside her head as she danced. She got lost in the music, in him, and her smile couldn't spread any wider across her face.

The music ended on a high note, and her head snapped up, coming within an inch of Coop's face. So close his scent became hers. So close if she'd tugged just a little bit on his neck, their lips would meet. She fell into the blue brilliance of his eyes, so inviting, as if to say *come, stay, be.*

If only.

Coop seemed lost too, his breaths ragged, his skin heated. He glanced at her mouth, and she parted her lips. He inhaled deeply and was about to bring his mouth to hers. But then he blinked. And in that blink, she saw his retreat. Saw the way his eyes hardened a bit. He was running. Backing off. She expected it.

And she wasn't giving up.

"I think I need some air." She waved her hand, fanning her face. Even though it was spring, she felt the heat down to her toes. "Take a walk with me?"

"Ah...sure. Just let me check on Cassie."

"Cassie is with your dad." She gestured to the photo booth. Cassie was wearing a purple feathered boa around her neck and had just wrapped Grandpa Joe up in a red one.

Coop laughed. "Better him than me."

"Well, we'd better make a run for it, before she nabs you too."

"Good idea." Coop placed his hand on her back and led her away from the party.

They walked past peach trees twinkling with starry lights to the orchards beyond, the golden hues of sunset guiding their way.

"I love it here," she said.

"The orchard is pretty darn beautiful this time of day. And you look just as beautiful, Taylor. I meant to tell you that earlier."

"But you were too busy avoiding me."

"I wasn't avoiding anyone," he said quietly.

Taylor's eyes narrowed. He was clueless how obvious he was. "Really? I thought we were friends?"

"We are. We're more than friends."

Her eyebrows went up. Was he finally admitting something?

"We're old friends."

She slugged him lightly in the arm. "Speak for yourself, old man."

"Now I'm an old man?"

"Well, you're thinking like one."

"This all started because I paid you a compliment."

She folded her arms across her middle. "I know. You shouldn't say things like that, unless…"

"Unless what?"

"Unless you plan on following through." She gazed at his mouth long enough to make her message ring loud and clear. "By the way, you look devastatingly handsome tonight, Coop." Then she skipped on ahead and picked a low-lying peach. She turned and tossed it to him. "Heads up, Coach."

Stunned, Coop barely caught the peach before it hit him in the shoulder.

Okay, so her aim wasn't the greatest. "Nice save."

Coop laughed and loosened his tie. It was twilight in the orchard now, the light so dim, she could hardly make out the peach coming at her. Surprised, she lowered her hands for a basket catch—thank you, Grandpa Joe, for the instruction—

and the peach dropped into her palms.

Coop's eyes nearly bugged out of his head. "Good catch, rookie."

"Thanks, sometimes I amaze myself."

He laughed again. "You always amaze me."

Taylor smiled. "Promise?"

He walked over to her. "Promise."

"Prove it." She inched closer to him.

"How?" They were almost nose to nose now.

Taylor opened his palm and placed the peach in his hand. "When life hands you a peach, make peach pie." Then she walked past him and headed back to the reception, hearing him grumbling about how that didn't make a lick of sense.

She grinned.

She wasn't giving up on Coop. Not by a long shot.

THE FIRST THING Coop thought about on Sunday morning was peaches. Full, ripe, beautiful on the inside and out, peaches. They'd plagued his mind last night too after the reception ended. And wouldn't you know it, his father had woken up and made them peaches and cream oatmeal for breakfast.

Peaches and Taylor.

Taylor and peaches.

He couldn't get away from the woman. He wasn't sure he wanted to, but could he forget how she'd broken his heart as a teen? Could he forgive himself for Francine's death? Could he risk putting Cassie's heart in jeopardy?

A knock came at his door, right at nine o'clock. He opened the door to Julie and Miguel and invited them into the house. "You two are up early," he said, surprised to see them.

"We can't stay but a minute," Julie said. "We're on the way to the airport. But I couldn't leave without thanking you in person for the she-shed again. And it's just perfect now, thanks to your thoughtful gift, Coop. That photo frame brought tears to my eyes." Julie walked into his arms and hugged him tight. "Now I'll always have a part of the gazebo. And those photos? It's insane how much I love them. I don't think I'll never forget your kindness, Coop. It really touched me."

"I'm glad. I'd hoped you would like it. Miguel helped me find the photos."

"He confessed." She put her hands on her hips. "You two are way too good at keeping secrets."

"Guilty as charged, Mrs. Herrera."

Julie beamed. "I love it when you call me that."

Cassie and his father walked up and greeted them with hugs.

"Cass, thank you again for being our flower girl," Julie said.

She nodded. "It was fun. Well, after a while…it was fun."

"You did great."

"Where's Taylor?" Cassie asked.

"Well, she's saying goodbye to her father. He's going to the airport later today. Then it'll just be Taylor and Muffy at the house for the next two weeks. I was hoping," Julie said, glancing from Cassie, to him, to Grandpa Joe, "that you could look in on her once in a while."

"Sure, we could do that!" Cassie jumped at the chance.

"Of course we'll have that gal over for dinner. Make sure she doesn't get lonely," his dad said.

Coop kept silent.

"Daddy, can we invite Taylor to my next game?"

All three of them were looking at him, more like ganging up on him. He paused for a second. There was no way out of this. No reason not to be neighborly. "I don't see why not."

"Yippee!" Cassie hugged Coop tightly around the waist, her head smashed up against his stomach. "Thanks, Daddy."

He ruffled the top of her hair. "Sure."

When he looked up, Miguel was eyeing him carefully. "Coop, can I have a private word with you?"

"Uh, sure. Let's step out back for a second."

"Now what are you two up to?" Julie asked, but it was good-naturedly.

"Don't worry, dear wife," Miguel said with a wink. "You'd approve."

Cassie took Julie by the hand. "Wanna see my school project? It's all about sloths. I got an A on it."

"I love sloths. And school projects."

"Yeah, because you're a teacher and all."

Coop left the three of them and walked outside with Miguel. Once out of earshot of his daughter, he asked, "What's up?" Though he had a pretty good idea.

"Listen man, I think we're pretty good friends, otherwise I wouldn't be butting in where I'm not wanted. But do you know what you're doing with Taylor?"

"Me? I'm not doing anything with Taylor."

"Exactly my point. She's a keeper, in case you haven't noticed."

Coop's skin prickled. "Should I notice?"

"Yeah, I think you should. Everybody knows what you've been through, Coop. But it's been years and maybe it's time for you to give yourself a break. Maybe it's time to take a risk. Taylor isn't going to break your heart again. She's not going to leave you high and dry."

"No? How can I be sure? Just think of what would happen to Cassie if she did?"

"Just think of what would happen to Cassie if she didn't?"

The man had a point. Cassie idolized Taylor. He'd pretty much bombed out keeping the two from forming a bond. In many cases, he'd unwittingly encouraged it. "Besides, you're talking as if Taylor was staying indefinitely. She's not. She's here only for two more weeks." And he'd miss her like crazy.

"Unless someone wakes up and stops her from leaving. She loves it here, Coop. And I think if you tried, you could convince her stay. Just saying..."

Coop stared at his friend. He was right. At least, he thought so. But was it the right thing to do?

Miguel shook his hand then and bid him farewell. He was off on a honeymoon with his new wife, the woman who made him the happiest.

Taylor made Coop happy. He couldn't deny it.

Suddenly, peaches entered his mind again.

When life hands you a peach, make peach pie.

Chapter Ten

AT THE SOUND of a knock, Muffy raced to the front door, barking like her life depended on it. It wasn't because she was such a good watchdog but because she was hoping to find Julie and Miguel on the other side. Her tail was wagging so hard her entire little body shook, waiting. Taylor felt sorry for her. Though they were pals, Muffy missed her true owners.

And it was only Tuesday. Of the first week.

"C'mon, Muffy. Let's get our pizza. I'll even give you some of the cheese."

Once the pizza delivery guy left, Muffy hung her head. It was true, Taylor had been super busy working on Nicole's gown and hadn't given Muffy enough attention. What she needed was a playmate. Someone who'd have time for the dog when Taylor was too busy concentrating. This gown had to be perfect, and she was hand sewing the bodice right now. Having the house to herself meant she didn't have to put everything away at night. Oh, she'd tidy up, but for the most part, she pretty much kept her workspace intact.

After dinner, Muffy set her head on her paws, her face

forlorn. Not even pizza cheese had perked her up.

Taylor couldn't take that sad face another minute. "Okay, Muff. You win. We're going out."

Taylor abandoned her work. And as soon as Muffy saw the leash in Taylor's hand, she bounded up, flapping her tail around like a windmill, creating quite a breeze. "Let's go, fluffball."

Taylor locked up the house and out they went, Muffy leading the way. Every ten feet or so, the dog stopped, stiffed, sometimes did her business and then was off again. Taylor didn't mind the pace. The air was fresh, the evening cooler than most. Before she knew it, Coop's house was in sight and she spotted Cassie outside on the front lawn throwing a baseball to her dad.

Muffy barked and she shushed her, but it was too late. Cassie turned around and started waving. She said something to her dad and he nodded.

Then Cassie came running over. "Hi," she said, out of breath.

"Hi, Cass. We're just going for a walk."

She nodded and bent down to Muffy's level. "Hi, Muffy." She stroked her behind the ears and Muffy rewarded her with doggie kisses. Cassie giggled.

"You're still gonna need a bath tonight, no matter how much Muffin cleans you up," Coop said, coming to stand beside Taylor.

"I know, Daddy." Cassie rolled her eyes. "She's kissing

me, not cleaning me."

Coop met her eyes and they both grinned. "Hey," he said. "Going for a walk?"

"Yes, Muffy decided we both needed to see the light of day, well, before the day ends."

"Working hard, huh?"

She nodded. "I tend to lose myself in my work."

"I get that."

"Only problem is, I feel sorry for Muffy. She's finding out, I'm no party."

Coop shook his head. "You're a party and a half, Taylor."

She stared at him for a second, noting his sincerity and warmth spread throughout her body. "Not according to the dog. I'm afraid I'm neglecting her. I think she could use a pal."

"Another dog?" he asked.

"Nope, just someone to come play with her."

"I could do it!" Cassie piped up. "Daddy, I could. I could go over after school."

Coop scratched his head. "Well, I don't know about that. What about practice?"

"That's only once a week."

"And your games. You have a game on Thursday. And your homework."

"Daddy, please, I promise I'll get it all done. It wouldn't be any different than when I came over to Julie's to help you after school. Only, this time, I'll be helping Taylor."

"I could walk her home," Taylor offered, liking this idea more and more.

Coop took a breath as he glanced at Taylor. "I have an idea. Why don't you come over for dinner tomorrow night? Bring Muffin for a trial run. We'll see how well Cassie and Muffin do together."

"Dinner?"

He nodded. "You know, when you open your mouth and put food in."

"You are so funny, Coop."

"So I've been told. Well?"

"Okay by me. What time?"

"Dinner is at six."

"That sounds good. I'll be there."

THE NEXT NIGHT, Grandpa Joe greeted her at his door at precisely six o'clock.

"Hi." She held Muffy in one arm and handed Joe a dish. "Marble pound cake, for dessert."

"Ah, thank you. Looks good."

As soon as Taylor set Muffy down, the dog began sniffing Joe's loafers, the floor and furniture. "Sorry about that. She'll settle down once she inspects the place."

"No problem. Muffy is welcome anytime. I like dogs."

"That's good to know."

"Cassie is finishing up her homework and Coop is getting washed up. Come in, dinner is almost ready."

"Thanks, something smells really good." The place had a garlicky aroma that invited her in and made her mouth water.

"Spinach lasagna. Gotta get Cassie to eat her veggies somehow. Trust me, you're gonna like it. Come into the kitchen. You can help with the salad."

"I'd love to." She liked the way Joe included her, rather than treating her like a guest. It had been that way for as long as she could remember.

In the kitchen, she cut up tomatoes and cucumbers, tore romaine lettuce, and made a simple dressing of olive oil and vinegar with herbs and Romano cheese.

"I see my dad's got you working the kitchen."

She looked up from her task at the island counter to find Coop, just out of the shower, she presumed, wearing a bicep-bulging T-shirt that said "Coach," smelling like soap and looking refreshed. His hair was still damp and combed off his face. She always found the locks curling at his nape pretty cute. Gosh, he'd hate that she thought that.

"I'm happy to do it."

Muffy was sniffing Coop and wagging her tail. He was more a sucker for this dog than he let on. "Dad went all out tonight. Lasagna. It's his personal best."

"Anything for our Taylor."

"Thanks, Joe," she said, humbled.

Coop picked up a piece of garlic toast and took a bite. After he chewed thoughtfully, he pointed to the basket. "Want one?"

"I'll wait until dinner." It was truly fascinating watching his throat work as he chewed.

When she was seventeen, she'd always loved watching Coop do anything. That much hadn't changed. She glanced at Joe at the stove and his eyes were on her, watching his son. He winked and heat rushed up her neck. She'd been caught and Joe had only smiled at her, nodding, telling her she wasn't fooling him. She put her head down and concentrated on finishing up the salad.

A minute later, Cassie breezed into the room. "Taylor, you're here!" Her welcome tugged at her heart and when the girl wrapped her arms around her and squeezed tight, she got a sense of what her life could be like every day, if she were truly a part of this family.

Unfortunately, she made the mistake of glancing at Coop. The downturn of his lips and the turmoil in his eyes killed the moment. Coop covered up nicely and put on a smile, but he wasn't good at hiding his emotions and protecting Cassie was first on his list.

"Cass, did you finish your homework?"

"Yes, Daddy."

"Good girl. Now, why don't you take Muffin and play with her in the other room. See how you two get along."

"Sure. C'mon, Muffy," she said, prancing into the other room with the dog at her heels.

"I have a feeling they'll do fine. But only if you think Cassie can handle it. I mean, with baseball and homework, it might be hard for her."

"Cass can handle it just fine, Taylor. Don't you worry. It's her dad who might have trouble,"

Joe replied.

"Uh…Pop? I think I can answer for myself." The look he gave Joe could stop a tiger in his tracks.

Taylor's lips twitched and then a rumble of laughter escaped. Why she found this all so amusing she didn't know, but rarely did Coop get put in his place. And Joe gave it to him good.

"You think it's funny?" He got in her face, his eyes piercing hers, and all she could do was continue to laugh. Then the sharpness in his eyes softened and his lips began to twitch too. It only took another moment for him to laugh it off.

"You never could stay mad at her," Joe interjected.

"Dad…"

"It's true, son. Face facts."

Coop sighed. "Isn't it time for dinner around here?"

"Coming right up," Joe said.

Joe and Taylor shared a grin and then put the food on the table, while Coop stood by, hands on hips, watching her set out plates and fill lemonade glasses.

Finally, he said, "I'll go get Cassie."

As soon as he was out of the room, Joe sidled up next to her and whispered, "I see the way you two are with each other. It's a shame my son is so pigheaded. I know he's got feelings for you. If you want an old codger's advice, I say stick with it. He's not a lost cause."

"Thanks for the advice. But just for the record, he's not giving me a reason to stay."

Joe put his hand on her shoulder. "Taylor, you don't need his permission. You can do what you want. Just think about it."

"I will, Joe. I will."

Actually, Joe was right. She didn't need to wait for Coop to come around. Her future was her future, and she was the one calling the shots. Joe had planted a bug in her ear. And, at the very least, it was worth looking into.

AFTER DINNER, JOE served the pound cake. "Yummy," Cassie said, taking a big bite.

There was milk for Cassie and Coop, while she and Joe chose to have coffee with their dessert. It was an easy time, for the most part, everyone relaxing and enjoying the cake. And, afterward, Taylor pitched in to do the dishes. Cassie cleared the table, while Joe washed and Taylor dried. Coop was designated to put everything away.

Taylor liked being a part of something bigger than her.

She hadn't had much sense of family in her life lately and being with the Coopers gave her an iota of peace, if not belonging. At times like these, she wished she'd had brothers and sisters, a whole family intact. But she loved her dad and promised to see him soon. She wouldn't break that promise. She'd already scheduled a long weekend trip to see him in two months, come rain or shine.

"Well, what do you think, Coop?" she asked.

He peered into her eyes and what she saw in his stopped her heart. He was always doing that to her, making mush of her brain with his potent looks, his mesmerizing stares.

"About what?" he said softly as she handed him a dish to put away.

"About…Cassie and Muffy?"

"Oh." He glanced away, thinking. "I suppose it'll work."

"Great. I think so too."

"She's got a game tomorrow though."

"And I promised to be there."

"So she can start on the next day."

"Daddy, really?" Eagle ears Cassie had picked up on their conversation and walked over, standing between them. "Can I see Muffy every day? And Taylor?"

"Yes, but remember, it's only temporary until Julie gets back. And not on game days. And only if you get all your homework done."

"I will, Daddy. I promise. And I won't break my promises. I'll be just like Taylor."

Coop squeezed his eyes shut for a second, and then recovered quickly, but she saw his doubt, his indecision in that moment. "Yeah, just like Taylor."

"I love you, Daddy."

"I love you too. Now, it's time for bed, Cass."

"I'll get her ready," Joe offered. "It's my turn and you know how much I like tucking her in."

"It's not your turn, Pop." Coop rolled his eyes. "But okay. Won't do to argue the point."

Taylor smiled at Joe. He was a matchmaking devil.

"Say good-night, Cassie, and don't forget to brush your teeth."

Cassie bid them goodbye and then gave each one of them a kiss, Muffy included. Grandpa Joe took Cassie's hand. "Good night, Taylor."

"Good night, and thanks again for dinner."

"Son, you be sure to take Taylor home now. The sun's gone down."

Once Joe was out of the room, she shook her head. "You don't have to take me home. Muffy's a good watchdog. I'll just walk home."

He pointed to Muffy, who was chewing on his shoelace. "That's like saying a corn dog is a gourmet meal."

"I like corn dogs."

"Not the point. C'mon. I'll walk you. It's a nice night."

"And I can burn off cake calories."

He gave her a once-over. "Like you need to."

Coop's compliment shot a ray of warmth to her belly.

"And you don't either, muscle man." She gazed at his biceps. They were hard to miss.

He laughed. "Muscle man? Is that anything like Superman?"

"You wish." She grinned.

"Oh, brother."

A minute later, they were outside strolling down the street. It was a short walk and they were comfortable just being quiet. Lots of somber thoughts were rolling around in her head, but Coop's presence beside her made her shove them all away.

Once they reached Julie's porch, she turned to Coop. "I had a nice time tonight. Thank you."

"I think Cassie was happiest of all."

She tilted her head. "Why do you always do that?"

"Do what?"

"Refuse to admit we can have a good time together?"

"I don't do that *all* the time."

She nodded. "Most of the time, you do. As if not admitting it will make it go away."

"Okay, I had a nice time with you tonight. Is that better?"

"Yes, a hundred times better."

"You make me forget, Taylor," he confessed, his beautiful mouth turning down. "And sometimes that's a dangerous thing."

"Are you talking about Francine? Or Cassie?"

"Both, I guess. It's been rough, being a single parent. Often, I had to hide my grief so Cassie wouldn't feel it. And, lately, I've been forgetting to remember Francine. I know that sounds crazy."

"It's not crazy at all. But, is it because of me?" she asked softly.

He nodded. "I think so. When you're around I feel good inside, but at the same time, I'm guilty. I worry about Cassie's young heart too."

"I get that. When I lost my mother, I wanted to hold on to all the memories, so she'd be alive in my heart forever. But even if my memories fade, my love for her won't. I figured that out a while back and it's really helped me."

He smiled then, and moved a strand of hair off her cheek. Even his slightest touch meant something profound to her. "That's because you're smarter than me."

"Am I?"

"Yeah, or else I wouldn't be doing this." And then his mouth covered hers, and the kiss surprised her and pulled her in at the same time.

A little moan escaped her lips as a thrill ran up and down her body. She could go on kissing Coop all night, but too soon, he backed away. Once her head cleared, she found him smiling at her. She blinked, smiling back, sure she wore a dreamy-eyed expression.

"I'd better wish you good-night."

She cleared her throat. "Yes…um, good night, Coop."

He started walking away, and when he was halfway down the street, he turned and waved.

She wiggled her fingers back, her heart full, and stared at him until he rounded the corner. The trouble was she understood what he was feeling. She understood his pain and doubt. It didn't make things easier knowing he was mentally keeping his distance from her. Every so often, he'd let his guard down and she would see the Coop she used to know.

She liked that Coop best of all.

Taylor took Muffy into the house and removed her leash. "There you go, girl, all free now."

Muffy turned around in circles, ten times at least, and then bounded into the kitchen for her meal. At least someone knew what they wanted.

She took a seat on the sofa, her mouth still tingling from Coop's kiss. She touched a finger to her upper lip and her eyes closed, remembering the glorious sensations. Not ten seconds later, her cell phone rang and she picked up immediately, wondering who'd be calling at this hour. It was Simone.

"Hi, hon. Is everything okay? It's almost midnight in New York."

"Yes, everything's okay. More than okay. Where have you been? I've been trying to reach you. I left you five voice mails."

"You did? Sorry, I didn't see them. I was at dinner with

friends."

"Well, hold on to your hat, I have something to confess and I hope you won't be too mad at me. Pretty, pretty please don't be mad." Her voice squeaked.

Taylor had never heard such a high-pitched plea coming out of Simone's mouth before. "Simone? What's going on?"

"Well, remember how you sent me your résumé to edit? Well, that sucker was in great shape and I…I sent it in under your name to Swivel Bridal along with your latest designs. And before you say anything, they loved, loved, loved your designs. They just got back to me…I mean you…today. And I thought I'd better tell you, before you saw it in your email."

"Simone, are you telling me you went behind my back, used my email account and sent in my résumé?"

"I did. I'm sorry. Is that horrible of me? I mean, I love your work and I knew this would be a perfect fit. Oh, please, forgive me. They want to do an interview with you ASAP."

"Simone, I can't just hop on a plane back to New York. I have obligations here."

"That's the best part, they love you so much, they're willing to interview you over the phone first. It's good news, right? I mean, it's what you've been hoping for. You'll be working for a company that appreciates you and your designs."

"I guess. I don't know. I, uh, I still can't believe you did this."

"But you'll forgive me. Please."

"Oh, for heaven's sake, Simone. I know your heart was in the right place. But now I'm going to have to think about this. How long do I have to get back to them?"

"I think ASAP does mean as soon as possible."

"Do me a favor? Don't respond for me again. I'll take it from here. I'll have to contact them tomorrow, I suppose."

"Are you angry with me?"

"I'm…neutral. But I can be pushed, so don't press your luck. And, Simone…thanks for believing in me."

"I always have."

They ended the call and Taylor sank into the sofa, stunned. Muffy picked up on her mood and jumped up, curling her body next to Taylor, all fluff and fur. She didn't have to ask herself why she wasn't jumping for joy right now. She should be on cloud nine. This was what she was hoping for. This was what she'd promised her mother. To have her dreams come true.

But was it what she truly wanted?

Dreams can change.

The image of Coop and Cassie at dinner tonight came to mind. If she landed this job, she wouldn't be any part of their lives anymore. It hurt to think it. But she knew the drill, all work and no play, if she wanted to further her career.

"I guess I have to see what this job is all about," she told Muffy. And with unusual reluctance, she opened her computer and read the Swivel email glowing with praise for her work.

ON FRIDAY, CASSIE showed up a bit early to play with Muffy. She'd had a half day of school and no homework. It worked out perfectly for Nicole's preliminary fitting. Muffy wouldn't get underfoot with Cassie keeping the dog busy.

"Nicole, what do you think?" Taylor asked as they both looked in the foyer mirror. "How does the material feel?"

"Oh, my gosh, this feels like heaven already. It's soft and the perfect color of rose."

"Okay, great. I'm pleased with it too, for now. I should have the gown ready ahead of schedule, if all goes well."

Nicole glanced in the mirror again. "You are so talented. This gown is very special and I'll never forget your kindness in agreeing to stay on, just to make it for me."

"It's what I do…what I love to do."

"Too bad you can't stay on here in Last Stand. We don't have a bridal salon and word of mouth of your work would spread like wildfire."

"You think so?"

"I do. We're a small town with a long grapevine reach."

"Well, I wish I could. But I've been offered a job in New York. It's a good offer, so I'm debating on taking it."

"That's good news for you, but bad news for Last Stand."

"It's bad news for me too." Cassie came into the room, her eyes misted with tears. "Are you leaving?"

Taylor forgot that Cassie had eagle ears. She and Muffy had been so quiet, Taylor thought they were in another part of the house. "Oh, uh."

"It's okay," Nicole said. "I'll go in and change out of my gown now. We're through, right? You two can talk."

And after Nicole left the room, Taylor took Cassie's hand leading her into the kitchen. "Have a seat, Cass."

She sat at the table and Taylor sat too, facing her, still holding her hand. "I didn't know you were leaving so soon," Cassie said.

"I didn't know either. And I haven't taken the job yet. I'm thinking it over."

"Does my dad know?"

Taylor blinked. "Your dad? No, he doesn't know. Not yet. Honey, you know I don't live here. You knew I was going to have to leave eventually."

"Yes, but you like it here and we all like you."

"I like you too. I'm sorry."

"It's okay." She put her head down. "I think I'll go home now."

"I'll walk you."

Cassie wasn't her jubilant self on the walk home. She kept her head down and didn't say a word. "You know, that single you hit yesterday was pretty awesome, you brought two runs in."

"Thanks."

"And that double play you made won you guys the game."

She shrugged. "I suppose."

A knot formed in Taylor's stomach. Cassie was hurting inside and it was her fault. She allowed the child to get close to her and maybe that was wrong, but it had happened organically. They'd become friends, and then more than friends, just like Taylor and her father. Now, she'd have to explain to Coop. He'd been right all along. Cassie did get hurt and it was the very last thing she wanted to have happen.

Once they reached the house, Taylor gave Cassie a big hug and the girl walked into the house. Taylor took a seat on the porch steps, her head down. She felt awful. The screen door opened and then flapped shut.

Coop took a seat beside her, their legs brushing. "Care to tell me what's up with my daughter? She walked in, went right to her bedroom, and threw herself on her bed. Sometimes, she's a drama queen, but I don't think that's it today."

"No, it's not. She's upset."

"Did she do something wrong?"

Taylor shook her head. "No, nothing like that. She overheard me talking to Nicole about a job offer I received from New York. I haven't accepted the job, but she got wind of it and well, she feels bad."

"Because you'll be leaving?"

Taylor sighed. "I told her I haven't made up my mind yet."

"Is it a good offer?" he asked.

"It's pretty much everything I'd want. More input. More trust in my designs. A small staff." She'd spent an hour on the telephone interview and it had gone better than she'd hoped.

"Wow," he said. "That sounds too good to pass up."

She turned to face him. As usual, his eyes gleamed as blue as a sun-drenched ocean. "I'm not sure what to do."

"Taye, if it's what you want, then you should take the offer."

But it wasn't what she wanted. What she wanted was sitting right next to her. But he still wasn't opening up. He had a battalion guarding his heart, and there was no crack in the armor, that she could see.

She sighed. "Maybe you're right."

Coop let out a long sigh too. "We'll miss you around here, that's for sure."

Taylor had no comeback for that. Missing her family and the Coopers was what she feared most. But she couldn't voice it, because she'd break down. And Coop didn't need to see her blubbering.

"Well, I'd best go check on Cass. Talk it out with her."

She nodded and rose too. "I'll be going now."

"Yeah, I know." Coop gave her a long look, as if to say he'd always known she'd be going, but that wasn't what she'd meant at all. He was just being annoying Coop again.

She stood there a minute ready to plead her case and make him see he had more to lose than to gain, by her leaving. But he wasn't giving an inch. He'd pretty much told her to take the job and go back to where she'd come from.

Taylor didn't muster her courage, didn't fight the good fight, she simply left his house and headed back to Julie's house.

She had an early dinner date with Blake Charles, and she didn't want to be late.

COOP POPPED HIS head into Cassie's room and found her lying on her bed looking at her favorite baseball book. Looking at, not really seeing it. Coop knew that numbing feeling too. And part of him was experiencing that now. Because Taylor was leaving.

"Hi, Cass."

She didn't look up from her book.

He walked inside and was taken with how his daughter's room was a mixture of little girl and true-blue baseball fan. She had dolls and furniture sitting in a dollhouse he'd built for her when she was four, one wall decorated with colorings and drawings she'd done since kindergarten. Her baseball mitt, balls and bats sat in one corner of the room with posters of her favorite Texas Rangers taped up on the space over her bed.

"Mind if I sit?" He took a seat on the edge of her bed. "You gonna tell me what's wrong?"

She sighed. Sometimes his eight-year-old daughter looked like the weight of the world rested on her shoulders. "Taylor is leaving."

"I know."

"She told you? She didn't think it would make a difference if you knew."

That stung. "I just found out, sweetheart. But I always knew she wouldn't stay."

"She said she doesn't live here. But she could. She could live here."

"She needs a job, Cass. There's a job waiting for her in New York."

"You don't want her to stay, do you, Daddy? I thought she was your friend."

Coop rubbed the back of his neck. A headache was coming on. There was too much crowding up in there, too much he'd been sorting through. And now, his daughter was making sense. Too much sense. "She is my friend."

"You like her, Daddy. I know you do."

"It's complicated, Cass."

"It's not that complicated," Joe chimed in.

His father had shown up in Cass's doorway, leaning his body against it and giving him a pointed look. Two against one.

"Dad, you're not helping," Coop said.

"Here, I thought I was." He winked at Cassie and she smiled.

Oh, man.

"Okay, enough said. I'm sorry you're disappointed, Cass, but sometimes we—" He stopped himself.

He couldn't tell his daughter that sometimes we don't get what we want. She'd lost her mother, someone who'd cuddle her at night, someone who would know to buy her dresses, someone to confide in about female things. Cass certainly hadn't gotten what *she* wanted in life. So, telling her that would cut into her still seeping wound.

He walked over to her and kissed her forehead. "I love you, Cass. It's going to be okay."

Cass only nodded and lifted her book again.

Thirty minutes later, Coop plopped his hat on his head, got in his truck and drove into town. He was determined to put a smile on his daughter's face today. He parked in front of Char Pie and stepped out of his truck. Taking his hat off, he breathed in cool fresh air. Summer would be here soon, but today was brilliant, the sky blue with no sign of Texas humidity. He heard footsteps on the sidewalk and a couple laughing, their laughter reaching over to him and as he pivoted around recognizing the female voice, he spotted Taylor being escorted into a restaurant with Blake.

Something twisted in his gut.

Taylor and Blake?

Whatever they were talking about sure made Taylor laugh.

Coop stuck his hat back on his head, pushed it down and barreled into the pie place.

"Hey, there." The cheerful girl behind the counter smiled. Why was everyone so darn happy around here? "How can I help you?"

Was there any help for him? He scoffed and looked at the pie shelves. "I'll take a cherry pie and one of those big, giant chocolate fudge brownies." The brownie was all for Cass. It was her favorite and she loved cherry pie too. So she could have some of that as well.

In the back of his mind, he knew this wasn't what Cassie wanted. But it was the best he could do at the moment. His head wasn't exactly clear.

Cheerful Christy packed up the items and sent him off with her big smile.

Once he got home, his dad offered up dinner, meatloaf and potatoes, not his best meal and they ate it in silence. "Hey, Cass, guess what I picked up today?"

"What's that?"

Coop walked over to the counter and opened up the bag. "Cherry pie and…your favorite." He pulled out the brownie and Cass's eyes grew wide for a few seconds.

"Thanks, Daddy."

"You're welcome, sweetheart."

"Want some now?"

She nodded, and he set the entire brownie in front of her. He was certain he was breaking half a dozen parenting rules right now. "Here you go."

"I think I'll skip cherry pie for now," his dad said.

"That's not like you, Pop. You okay?"

"Fine, son. Just gonna rest up a bit."

"Okay, Dad. I'll get the dishes tonight."

"I appreciate that."

"Grandpa? What's wrong?" Cassie walked over to him, concern bringing the corners of her mouth down.

"Nothing, honey. I'm fit as a fiddle. Just didn't sleep too well last night, is all." He patted Cassie's head and kissed her forehead. "I'll be fine."

An hour later, Coop sat down at his drafting table, working on major plans to renovate the Barton ranch house about three miles up the road. The job would take him into the fall months and he'd have to use his entire crew to finish it on time. He was glad for the steady work and really had no complaints about his professional life. At least that wasn't suffering.

Nor was his appetite. He'd dug into that cherry pie tonight like there was no tomorrow. Now his stomach rebelled. He put his pencil down and sipped coffee. He had an odd feeling tonight and it wasn't just about Cassie or seeing Taylor with Blake, it was about his dad.

Joe had always been Coop's rock. A man's man. The guy was strong and stout. He'd never shown an inkling of weakness. But, lately, Coop had noticed him slowing way down. He tired easily and often he'd look pale.

His cell phone rang, making him jerk in his chair. He answered it quickly. "Hello."

"Hi, it's me."

"Taylor?" Her sweet voice rang in his ears. She usually didn't call him. "What's up? Is everything okay?"

"Well, not really. I think I need some help."

"Why, what's wrong?"

"A pipe broke under the sink, and I don't know how to shut the water off. It's leaking all over the kitchen."

"Hang on, I'll be right over."

TAYLOR WAS KEEPING an eye out for Coop. She felt so helpless. She didn't know where the main shut off valve was, and she had no clue what to do about a pipe breaking. Maybe she should've called a plumber, but as soon as it happened, Coop's image popped into her head and he was the first one she'd called.

His truck pulled up in less than five minutes. She stood at the opened door, but he ignored her initially and ran right to a water outlet hidden behind the bushes backing up against the house. He took some time back there, but when he appeared, he nodded his head. "I shut off the main water valve."

"Thanks for coming over so quickly."

"I'm not far. But, hey, you're drenched."

She was. Her hair and face got soaked as she was trying to contain the leak under the sink. The rest of her clothes, her jeans and blouse were saturated. She'd put on a hooded jacket to cover up, but there was no denying she looked like a water rat.

"The kitchen's a mess. I feel so bad." She led him inside to the kitchen.

"Hey, it's not your fault. This stuff happens all the time." He assessed the damage looking around with expert eyes, bending down to see under the sink.

The floor was soaked everywhere they stepped, but she didn't think the cabinets or the counters were involved.

"Well, we'll sop up what we can for now. Then find set up fans to dry out the floor."

"You don't have to do that," she said. "I can manage. You must've been busy when I called."

"I wasn't on a date with Blake Charles, like you were."

Her brows lifted. How did he know that? Puzzled, she opened her mouth to speak but he was quicker.

"I saw you two in town together. Going into a restaurant." His voice was light but accusation entered his eyes, giving him away.

"It wasn't really a date. We had things to discuss and we decided to do it over dinner."

"If you say so. You two looked awfully chummy."

"But then I called you when I needed help," she pointed out.

"I live closer."

"You know that's not the reason."

His smile said he did.

Taylor went into the linen closet and pulled out a bunch of towels. "Well, might as well get started on this."

"You sop and I'll try to fix the pipe."

"You can do that?"

"With tape I can. I have it in the truck. It'll be temporary, until the pipe can be replaced. Which I can do tomorrow, if you want."

"You'd do that for me?"

His head tilted to the side and the look he gave her said she was crazy to ask.

Okay, so if nothing else, he was still her best friend.

An hour later, after cleaning up the kitchen and having a cup of coffee together, Coop rose from the table. "It's late. I need my beauty sleep."

She laughed, because it really was funny. Coop was one of the most masculine, appealing men she'd ever known. He wasn't pretty, except for his striking eyes, yet he had the kind of rugged good looks most women dream about.

She rose as well and walked him to the door. "I can't thank you enough. I'm sure Julie and Miguel appreciate your fast action in saving the house."

"All in a day's work."

He winked and that one gesture gave her the courage to reach up and kiss his cheek. "Thanks again. I mean it."

Their eyes met for a few lingering seconds and then he nodded. "I'll be by in the morning around nine to see about replacing the pipe. Don't call a plumber just yet."

"Sounds good." It really did. She'd have coffee and muffins waiting for him.

He bid her good-night, walked to his truck, started the engine and then waved to her before taking off.

BY 9:30 THE next morning, Taylor paced the kitchen floor. The faux wood was almost dry, thanks to two box fans she'd set out last night. Banana chip muffins were waiting and freshly brewed coffee was keeping warm in the coffeemaker. Where was Coop? He'd said nine o'clock. Had something come up with his work? Or had he forgotten about her?

She made herself busy by scrubbing the kitchen counters until they sparkled and then checked drawers and cabinets, making sure she hadn't missed any water damage. Whenever she got antsy, she would clean. It kept her nerves at bay, kept her hands busy and kept her mind from going to crazy places. Yep, Taylor could scrub like the best of them.

Once she was through, she gave the kitchen a good long look. Goodness, the damage could've been much worse. She felt responsible for the house in Julie's absence and it was all fine and good, until something like this happened. Even Muffy seemed to know something was off. She hadn't made an appearance in the kitchen since it all happened.

Her cell phone rang, but the tone was muffled. She searched the kitchen, sure she'd brought it in here earlier. And on the fourth ring, she finally figured out the ring was coming from the top drawer by the sink. She must've dropped it in there accidentally this morning while she was cleaning. She grabbed it quickly, hoping to catch whoever was on the other end. "Hello? Hello?"

"Taylor?"

Coop's voice was low, pained, and she pushed the phone closer to her ear. "What is it? What's wrong?"

She knew him. Knew when he wasn't himself. He sounded somber, bleak. It hurt her heart.

"It's my dad. He's in the hospital."

"Joe? Oh, no." She clutched her chest, totally not expecting this. "What happened?"

"I found him on the floor near the kitchen door. He was on his way to make coffee when his legs buckled under him. He clunked his head pretty hard on the floor too. I drove him to the emergency room. He's being tested now. He was pretty weak."

"I am so sorry. Poor Joe. What can I do?"

"Nothing really."

"Where's Cassie?"

"She's in school right now. She doesn't know anything

about this. She'll be upset, for sure. She and my dad are close."

"I'm coming to the hospital," she announced.

"You don't need to do that."

She wasn't about to let him push her away. He needed her, and so did Grandpa Joe. "I'm coming, end of story."

"Okay...thanks."

She hung up the phone, packed up the muffins and told the real Muffin, "Stay."

Muffy hated being left behind but this time she obeyed and stayed put with her head down as she watched Taylor walk out the door.

She drove to Jamison Hospital on the edge of town and found Coop pacing in the waiting room on the third floor. As soon as he spotted her, relief flooded his eyes and he put out his arms. She walked straight into them, hugging him tight. She was glad she'd come. It was obvious Coop was worried out of his mind. "How is he?" she asked as she pulled away.

Coop shrugged. "It wasn't a heart attack, so that's a relief. They are still doing tests, but it looks like a classic case of dehydration. Apparently, he's being grouchy, which tells me he's feeling better."

"That is a good sign. Coop, I'm so sorry this happened."

"Yeah, well, Dad's getting up in age. It's time he realized his limitations."

"Nobody really wants to do that, do they?"

"I guess not. I'm going to have to be diligent with him. I mean, it's just the three of us. We're a unit. And we need to stay that way. Cassie can't lose—"

He didn't finish the thought but Taylor knew what he meant. Cassie can't lose anyone else she loved. She squeezed his hands. "She won't, Coop. Your dad should make a full recovery."

Taylor persuaded Coop to sit down. She offered him banana chip muffins and served him coffee from the pot in the waiting room. They sipped coffee, sat together, holding hands and an hour later, Coop got the diagnosis from Joe's attending doctor. Exhaustion and dehydration. He would stay overnight and they'd take it from there.

"I don't know what to tell Cassie," he said.

"Tell her the truth. Her grandpa is doing too much and needs to rest and drink a lot more liquids. He needs to slow down. He has to take his retirement seriously. And if he does all that, he'll be fine."

"She'll be worried."

"She's a bright girl. She'll handle it, Coop. You have to give her room to grow up. You can't protect her from everything," she said softly.

He slipped his hand from hers to scrub his face, and then let go a weary sigh. "She's been through a lot."

"Of course she has. And so have you. No one is denying that."

"I don't want her to have another moment of grief."

"I get that. Listen, why don't I stay here while you go pick up Cassie from school later on. You can explain what happened to her. And this way, Grandpa Joe, won't be alone."

He turned his wrist, glanced at his watch. "That's not for another two hours. You don't have to sit here with me all that time. Don't you have a gown to work on?"

"It's almost finished. And I want to see Joe. It's no imposition."

Didn't he know she cared about his entire family? She wasn't going to let him go through this all alone. He was *her guy*. Even if he had no clue about her true feelings, she needed to be here. To see him through this. It wouldn't feel right being anywhere else.

COOP STOOD BESIDE his truck waiting for Cassie to stroll out of the school gate. At the sight of him, her eyes lit up. Just like every day. He'd never tire of seeing her bright eyes and sunny expression when he picked her up from school. But today, his stomach was in knots.

She ran over to him and gave him a hug around the waist. He held on to her extra tight this time. This wasn't going to be an easy conversation, but he'd take Taylor's advice and tell her the truth, without too much sugarcoating.

"Hi, Daddy."

"Hey, Cass. How was school?"

She gave him her usual, "Okay."

He smiled and grabbed her backpack as she climbed into the truck. After they were seated and she was latched into her seatbelt, he looked over at her. "Cass, I have something to tell you. Grandpa Joe is going to be fine, but he took a little fall today and I had to take him to the hospital."

"Grandpa's in the hospital?"

Coop held back his cringe. Cassie's expression had gone from happy to worried in a split second. "Why? Is he going to be okay? What happened to him, Daddy?" Tears welled in her eyes.

Coop's gut twisted even more. "He's a little bit weak right now. He wasn't drinking enough and he was working too hard. So, the doctor said we, meaning you and me, have to make sure he gets enough fluids and takes it easier. You think you can help me do that?"

"Yes, Daddy." She bobbed her head up and down. "I can do that. Starting tonight."

"Well, Grandpa's not coming home tonight. He'll rest up in the hospital and come home, hopefully tomorrow."

"Can I see him?"

"Yes, how about we head over there now. Taylor was nice enough to stay at the hospital with him, so he wouldn't be alone."

"That's because Taylor *is* nice, Daddy."

"Tell me something I don't know." He winked.

But his daughter wasn't buying his good mood. She was petrified. Worried about her grandpa.

Once they arrived at the hospital, Cassie got out of the truck and stood frozen for a moment, staring at the large looming building. He could almost read her thoughts—Grandpa shouldn't be here. He belonged at home with her.

"Cass, it's going to be okay."

Her voice cracked. "H-how can you be so s-sure, Daddy? Mommy was in a hospital and she never came home."

Coop sucked in a breath. His emotions were a wreck, but he held strong for her sake. "Because it's different, Cass. You're just gonna have to trust me."

She took his hand. Together they made their way into the hospital and rode the elevator up to the third floor. They found his father, sitting up, conversing with Taylor. Both had smiles on their faces. If anyone could make his dad smile, it was Taylor. She had a natural rapport with him that, at times, Coop envied.

"Grandpa!" Cassie rushed over to the bed and looked him over from his head down to the toes hidden underneath the bedsheets. Tears welled in her eyes seeing him hooked up to machines and tubes.

"Hello, sweetie. How's my big girl doing?"

His father's voice echoed against the walls, an obvious overcompensation for Cassie's sake.

Cassie glanced at Taylor, who sat on a chair pulled up next to the bed. Taylor gave her a reassuring nod. "I'm fine,

Grandpa. But what about you?"

"Me? I'm doing better now that the doctors got a hold of me. I'll be tip-top and coming home soon."

"Daddy said you have to stay here tonight."

"I do. They want to make sure all my bells and whistles are in working order. Which they are, so I'll be home before you know it, sweetheart."

Cassie didn't look so sure.

"Climb up on the bed and give Grandpa a big kiss. Right here." He pointed to his cheek. "That's the best medicine of all."

Cassie did just that and his dad closed his eyes, absorbing all her love. Then she climbed down, and grabbed on to his hand.

"Don't you worry about me," he told her straight out. "I'm not going to miss a one of your baseball games."

Cassie chuckled a bit.

"Cass, how about you keep Grandpa company while I talk to Taylor outside," he said.

"Okay, Daddy."

Taylor rose from her chair. "Joe, it's good to see you feeling better."

"Your visit had a lot to do with it. I appreciate it."

"Of course. You just get better now. I know Cassie will watch over you carefully." She bent to kiss his cheek. The old man blushed and Coop had to admit, Taylor sure had a way about her.

"Okay, enough of that," Coop said.

"My son's jealous."

"I doubt that," she said, smiling.

"Don't doubt it, Taylor. It's a fact."

"Glad to see you've got your ego back, Dad."

"Never lost it." He winked at Taylor.

Coop shook his head. Then he put his hand to Taylor's back and led her out of the room. Once they were in the hallway, Coop stopped to face her. "Thanks for this, Taylor. I appreciate your help with my dad. Sorry I didn't get over to fix that pipe for you."

"You had more important things to do. I'll call a plumber."

He nodded. "You're good in a crisis."

"I am?"

"Yeah, you kept me calm, and—"

"Held your hand."

"You did that too and kept my mind off, well, certain things."

"Don't forget the muffins I baked. I mean, as long as you're complimenting me, might as well get it all in."

"Right, you make a mean banana muffin, lady."

"I know."

"I, uh, took your advice about telling Cassie the truth. She was upset, but it was the right thing to do."

"She would've known if you tried to cover it up anyway. She's a smart girl. And I'm sure you're both relieved it wasn't anything real serious."

"Yep, that'd be right." Coop sighed and rubbed the back of his neck, thinking. This is where it got real sticky. He had to say goodbye to Taylor. She'd be leaving soon anyway. "So when do you go back to New York?" he asked.

She blinked, and color drained from her face. "What?"

"You know, that dream job you were offered. You are taking it, aren't you?"

"Oh, um, I haven't promised them anything yet."

"No?"

"No." She shook her head and all that dark lush hair moved over her shoulders.

"I thought for sure you'd snap it up."

"Is there a reason I shouldn't snap it up?" Hope filled her eyes and her smile awaited a return.

"I mean, are you giving me a reason?"

Oh, God. This was what he feared. He didn't want to hurt Taylor. She was amazing, and he probably was deeply in love with her, but he couldn't chance it. He couldn't trust that she'd stay this time. That she wouldn't resent him for holding her back from her dream. If she left, it would crush him and devastate Cassie. "I can't, Taye. You saw how Cassie was with my father. She's worried sick over him. And if you and me didn't work out, Cassie would bear the brunt of it. She's already been hurt so much. She couldn't stand to lose someone else in her life."

"So, it's better to just exist? And not really live? There are no guarantees in life, Coop. Remember that. Every time we step outside, we take a risk. Only you won't take one on me."

"It's not that, Taylor."

She backed up a step and shook her head. "I hope you get what you want out of life, Coop. I really, really do."

Then she turned and walked away. He watched her until she disappeared down the hospital corridor. There was no doubt she was out of his life now.

He'd pushed her away as hard as he could.

Tears formed behind his eyes.

And every cell in his body ached from the loss.

TWO DAYS LATER, Nicole stood facing her reflection in the mirror at Julie's house, a big grin on her face. Lindsey stood on one side of her and Taylor stood on the other scrutinizing the pale rose wedding gown. It was the final fitting and Taylor scrutinized her work with an expert eye. She'd put her heart and soul in this gown, and she was happy with the results. The fabric, lace overlay and cut of the gown suited Nicole to a T.

"It's beautiful, Taylor. Just like I'd envisioned it and worth every penny. How can I ever thank you?"

"Just wear the dress in good health, Nicole. That's all I want."

Funny, she'd never thought of designing wedding gowns to be so ironic. She made other women look gorgeous on their wedding day, but Taylor wasn't to have her own happy ending. She'd never design a gown for herself, even though she already knew exactly how she'd create it. The picture was clear in her mind.

"Hmm, I think I'm jealous," Lindsey said good-naturedly. "You get a one-of-a-kind wedding gown, Nic. And it's perfect on you."

"Thanks," she gushed, an infectious smile spreading across her face. "I think so too."

"Well, then. All you girls have to do now is walk down the aisle."

"It's coming so fast, I can hardly believe it." Nicole's mouth formed into a pout. "I sure wish you'd stay on, I'd love to have you come to my wedding."

"So would I," Lindsey said. "You're getting an invitation anyway."

"I'll track you down in New York, if I have to," Nicole added.

The girls welcomed her with such warmth, it almost made her forget her problems and the heartbreak that was wrapped up in one stubborn Texan. "You guys are gonna make me cry."

A group hug came next, all three of them tearing up and being super careful not to crush the dress.

"Are you leaving as soon as Julie gets back?" Lindsey

asked.

"I'm afraid so. I do have a job waiting for me."

"You do? So you took the position?" Nicole asked.

"Not yet, but I'm going to. I have no choice."

Nicole and Lindsey exchanged glances. Then Nicole pursed her lips. "Someone ought to hit that Coop over the head with a baseball bat. Wake him up a bit."

It was so unexpected, they all laughed. But the truth was, Taylor had put herself out there with Coop a couple of days ago and he'd rejected her. Her pride could only take so much. Nobody had to hit *her* over the head to figure he wasn't going to change his mind.

"I will be back, though. I'm determined to see my family more. Job or no job, I'm not going to let my career get in the way of seeing the ones I love."

"That's great," Lindsey said. "So, we'll be seeing you?"

"Yes, I promise."

"Well, a promise from you is good as gold."

And it was. She was only sorry she couldn't follow through on a crazy notion she'd had to buy the Purple Pansy and make a life here in Last Stand. Blake had put the bug in her ear, and she'd let the idea simmer in the back of her mind. But she couldn't live in the same small town with Coop and not be welcomed as a part of his life. It would be too hard. So that notion was only a wistful dream that had blown away with the slightest little gust.

ON SATURDAY AFTERNOON, Julie and Miguel returned from their honeymoon. After a round of hugs and kisses, they took a seat in the living room where the newlyweds shared fun stories about the islands. Taylor was happy for them, they were the perfect complement to each other and it was good to see Julie and Miguel's love shining so bright. But their homecoming was bittersweet because tomorrow Taylor would be leaving. It felt like not only would she be saying goodbye to her cousins, she'd be leaving the town she'd grown to love all over again.

Julie and Miguel lavished her with a water pearl necklace, a floral beach cover-up and plumeria-scented bath oils and lotions. Muffy wasn't left out either in the gift department, they'd brought her pineapple- and banana-shaped chew toys.

"Thank you both," she said, taking a whiff of the flower-scented lotion. "You know me so well. These are things I will definitely use, but it's too much."

"It's not too much," Julie said. "Not compared to what you've done for us, coming early to the wedding, being the best maid of honor ever, helping my friends with their wedding gowns, and then watching the house and Muffy while we were gone. I hate the thought of you leaving."

"I do too," Miguel said. "It's nice to have family around, you especially."

"Ah, thank you. I really have mixed emotions too. I'll be

going back to my life in New York, but I'll be leaving so much behind too."

"You promised to come back to visit, right?"

"Yes, I did and I will. And you can come up to New York for a girls' weekend."

"Sounds like fun. I'll do that. I guess I don't feel horrible now that I have your promise you'll visit more. And you've got that brand-new job waiting for you."

"Yes, I do."

"You don't sound happy, honey."

"I…am." She couldn't fake any enthusiasm.

Julie sensed her mood and hugged her tight. "Remember I'm only a phone call away."

She nodded, grateful for the comfort. "I know."

"How about we all go out to dinner tonight?" Miguel said cheerfully to change the mood.

"No way," she told him. "You two must be exhausted. I made dinner for all of us. And it'll be done in an hour so you guys have a chance to rest and get settled in."

"You didn't need to cook, hon."

"Hey, after I finished Nicole's gown, I had nothing but time on my hands."

She didn't go to Cassie's game yesterday and it had bothered her all day. According to Coop, the bond she'd developed with his daughter could stand to hurt her. And that was the last thing she wanted to do.

The roast she cooked came out a bit overdone and the

potatoes were not nearly as tender as she'd hoped, but the chocolate chip oatmeal cookies were pure perfection, so all was not lost. Still, Julie and her hubby were good sports about the meal and they tried to keep her spirits up as they dug into the food.

After dinner, Taylor excused herself to begin packing. In her room, she gathered up her belongings and stuffed them into the suitcases rather haphazardly. It was so unlike her, but she didn't care about wrinkles right now. She had other issues. She sank down onto the bed and closed her eyes. She couldn't leave town without saying goodbye to the Coopers. It was one stop she had to make, one stop she couldn't neglect as images of a recuperating Joe came to mind. And of Cassie, the adorable blond-haired tomboy she'd befriended, and then there was Coop.

The man had gotten under her skin. He'd been her white knight on so many occasions since she'd come to Last Stand. He'd come to her rescue when Muffy escaped on the first day she'd arrived in town. He'd carried her to safety after she'd been beaned by the baseball at Cassie's game. Then more recently, he'd raced over when she'd called for help when Julie's kitchen was flooding.

Coop was deadly handsome in a purely Texan way, tall and broad with blue eyes she could swim in. No New Yorker could rival his appeal. But all that didn't matter anymore. It couldn't. She didn't have a claim on his heart and she never would. This last visit would be painful, and yet, she had to do it. Had to see them all one last time.

Taylor covered a plate of oatmeal chocolate chip cookies wondering if it was a coincidence or a mechanism of her subconscious that compelled her to bake Coop's favorite cookies today. Whatever it was, Cassie would welcome them too, so Taylor hung on to that thought as she grabbed her leather bomber jacket and wished Julie and Miguel a good night.

Stepping outside, she took a giant gulp of air before heading toward the Cooper home. This was her last night in town and the walk would do her good. The sun was just disappearing on the horizon as dusk fell over the land, her favorite time of day. Before long she was facing the Cooper front door. One knock, then two.

Grandpa Joe opened the door, looking better than when she'd seen him in the hospital. "Hello, Taylor girl. This is a nice surprise. Come in."

"Hi, Joe. You're looking well."

"I'm feeling myself again. Got two hound dogs on my case if I don't."

He stepped aside so she could enter. "What'd you make me?" he asked.

"Cookies." She lifted the foil and showed him.

"Mmm, all for me?"

"No way, Dad. You get one." Coop walked over. "Doctor said you need to slim down a little."

He was speaking to his father, but his beautiful deep gaze

landed on her. She swooned a little, and then caught herself. He'd let his facial scruff grow into a full-fledged beard making those darn blue eyes really pop.

"You see what I mean, hound dog." Joe aimed his comment at Coop.

But Coop's eyes remained on her. "Hi," he said.

"Hi."

"Well," Joe said, "don't just leave her standing here, invite her in."

"No, no. It's okay. I'm not here to visit. I came to say…goodbye."

Coop took a swallow and blinked.

Joe gave his son a disgusted look, took the plate from her hands and shoved them at Coop. "Here, she made your favorite."

Coop stared down at the plate like it would solve the mysteries of the universe.

And then Cassie came running over, gripping her around the waist. "No, no. You're not leaving, Taylor. You can't."

"Cass." Coop put his hand on her shoulder and spoke softly. "We talked about this."

Taylor bent down to her level, her throat tight. "I'm sorry, Cassie. Really. But remember, we'll always be friends. If your daddy says it's okay, we can FaceTime together and I'll be back from time to time."

"It won't be the same," she said, staring straight into her eyes. "It just won't."

She couldn't lie to the child. "No, it won't be exactly the same."

Tears spilled down Cassie's cheeks. "I'm gonna miss you."

"We all will," Joe said.

Taylor rose then, because there wasn't much else to say. She gave Joe a big bear hug that lasted a long time. "Bye, Joe. You stay healthy now."

"Plan to."

She kissed Cassie's tearstained cheek. And a knot formed in her belly. This was harder than she thought. "Talk to you soon, Cass. I promise."

The girl nodded, but said nothing more.

"C'mon. I'll walk you outside," Coop said.

It was better to make a quick exit. "Okay."

She turned and Coop guided her outside, his hand to her back. Once out of earshot of the others, she turned. "Well, it's back to New York for me."

"Seems like you just got here," Coop said. "But it also feels like you never left."

"It's only been a few weeks, but I…"

"Yeah, I know." He gave her a sad smile. "So, you took the job?"

"Yeah, I did."

"It's gonna be good for—"

"Daddy, wait!" Cassie bounded out of the house, her hands behind her back as she ran toward them.

"Cass?"

She stopped up short when she reached them, out of breath. "Daddy, just listen to me. Please. And I hope you don't ground me for snooping. But if you do, it'll be worth it."

"What are you talking about, Cass? And what do you have behind your back?"

Cassie took a second to move, and then slowly put her palms out and unveiled what she held in her hands.

A walnut-stained wooden box, a little smaller than a cigar box with the initials TP and RC carved into the wood.

Stunned, Taylor stared at the box that had grown up with her. The box that had united her to Coop since childhood.

"Cassie, you did go snooping." Coop's voice held a dangerous edge. "Did you open it?"

"No, Daddy. I promise. But Grandpa told me about your promises to each other and I think there's one in there still. I think Taylor shouldn't leave until she sees what it is."

Coop's shoulders fell as if he was being hit by all sides.

"Can I see the box, Cassie?" she asked.

Carefully, Cassie put it in her hands.

"Thanks."

"I think you should go inside, young lady," Coop said, more bark than bite. She didn't think Cass was shaking in her boots. "I'll deal with you later."

"Okay, Daddy. But please, please open it."

Cassie had such hope on her face. And such love. She really was a special child. Once she walked into the house, Taylor studied the box for a few seconds and then turned to him. "You've had it all this time?"

"No. One of my crew found it when we were demolishing the gazebo. I, uh, I didn't think it would be wise to—"

"Technically it's mine, Coop. You promised to make it for me and you did."

"I know."

"I loved this box. I loved what it signified."

"Yeah, we had a pretty great friendship."

"Those promises kept us bonded. Remember when you promised me you'd learn how to bake cookies? I think you were ten or eleven."

"And I did, for that one year but then I forgot everything I learned. I had more fun eating them than baking them. I remember making you promise to watch all the Star Wars movies."

"Yes, and now I'm a fan. I've seen them all a bunch of times. Do you remember when you promised me you'd hit ten home runs during your baseball season?"

"I didn't hit ten." He grinned and his face lit up. "I hit twelve."

"Overachiever."

"I remember you promising to build me a snowman."

"I named it Coop."

"I still have that picture. You were standing right next to

it wearing a bulky red sweater with a big smile on your face."

"You still have it? That's sweet."

"What wasn't sweet was you making me promise to wear my dad's boots to school for a whole week. I nearly broke my neck falling out of them, but I did it. Sent you the pictures and Dad confirmed it that next summer."

"I only did that to get back at you for making me promise to dye my hair purple and keep it that way for a whole week. My mom wasn't too keen on that and I caught a lot of grief at school from my friends. And teachers."

"That was when you were fifteen, right?"

"Yeah, but it was kinda fun being the girl everyone noticed in school."

Coop lifted a strand of her long dark hair and eyed it with appreciation. "You were noticed, Taye. Even without purple hair, I noticed you."

"I, uh, noticed you too. Especially that last year. My mom always believed it was young love, more infatuation than anything else…but it was real for me."

"For me too. You were my first girl."

"You were my first guy."

"A lot of time has passed."

"Yeah."

"Coop, if I asked you a question, will you give me an honest answer?"

He inhaled and stared into her eyes. "Yeah, I will."

"Have you opened the promise box? Have you seen our

last promise to each other?"

He shook his head. "No. I didn't open the box."

"Why?"

"Because we always did it together."

"Well, we're here now."

"Yeah, we are and it's time," he said on a deep sigh. "You can go first."

Coop unlatched the box and opened the lid. He reached inside and lifted out the rolled-up paper marked with her handwriting and handed it to her.

She read the words silently first, her nerves strung tight. This was a baring of her soul and she needed a moment to herself. Tears stung her eyes. She remembered the emotion behind the words of her first and *only* declaration to any guy. "It's says, 'I promise to never stop loving you.'" She looked into his eyes and found softness there and affection. It helped her go on. "And I haven't, Coop. I've never really stopped loving you."

It explained the lousy dates she'd gone on, the way no guy had ever measured up. Thinking back on it now, she couldn't picture herself with any other man.

"Taye." Coop gulped air, his eyes on the verge of tears.

She waited patiently as he dipped into the promise box, coming out with the note and something else rolled up inside.

He unrolled it and read the words without hesitation. "It says, 'You're one of a kind, Taylor, and I promise to love you forever.'" Then he laid a delicate gold brooch designed with tiny roses into her palm and closed her hand around it. "This was my mother's. It's very special to me and I've always wanted you to have it. Because I love you, Taylor. I loved you then and I love you now."

"You do?"

"Took me a while to realize it, but I do, Taye. I love you. Cassie was right to snoop. She was right to bring out the promise box. That girl may not even get grounded. And Dad, well, he's quite a fan of yours. He said I've been a jerk to you. I know I have. I've fought my feelings for you since you got here. You know all the reasons, but I was wrong to deny us a second chance and I promise to make it up to you if you can ever forgive me." He took hold of her hands, and his eyes filled with so much regret she didn't doubt his sincerity for a second.

"For being cautious with your heart and protective of your daughter? I get that, I really do. Yes, Coop. I promise you're forgiven."

"Thank God." He closed his eyes briefly and then when he gazed at her again, she saw love on his face, in his eyes. It was a beautiful thing.

"And will you stay in Last Stand, Taylor? With me, us? Do you think you could be happy here?"

She clutched the rose brooch to her chest and answered without hesitation. "Yes, Coop. I *know* I'll be happy here."

"But your job?"

"Doesn't matter. I once promised my mother I'd pursue my dream and never give up on it. But what I found is that dreams change. And this dream, this promise, is the most important one in my life. That's all my mom wanted for me. To be happy in whatever I do."

"I love you, Taylor. With all my heart."

His words sank in and planted joy in places that were once hollow and empty. "I love you too, Coop. With all my heart."

Coop took her face in his hands, looked into her eyes and then lowered his head to brush his lips to hers. She slipped her arms around his neck as he deepened the kiss.

It was the kind of kiss a girl could only dream about.

And the kind of kiss that promised a lifetime of happiness.

Six months later...

AUTUMN LEAVES COLORED the earth and gentle breezes whisked away the humid remnants of summer. It was a perfect day for a wedding. Only this time, Taylor was the bride. She faced Coop in his backyard in front of the pristine new gazebo he'd constructed for her, for them. It was a symbol of their love and commitment. It was their childhood and their future. Maybe one day, their children would commandeer a pirate ship or set up a restaurant inside the white lattice walls of the gazebo.

Oh, how she loved the man she was to marry today. Dressed in an elegant black suit and string tie, he was a stunning groom.

Grandpa Joe stood by his side.

Julie stood by her side.

And little Cassie once again displayed her super flower girl powers wearing a dress that sparkled in the sunlight, her blond curls draping over her shoulders, a look of pure joy on her face.

Their friends and family were all here, Simone and Brenda making the trip from New York and her father standing on the steps of the gazebo, ready to marry them.

She wore her dream dress, an ivory gown of her own design with layers of delicate lace at the bodice gathered together by a very special golden brooch of tiny roses. Coop had noticed it and approval gleamed in his eyes.

"You look beautiful," Coop whispered for her ears only. "I can't wait to make you my wife."

"And I can't wait to call you husband."

And when the ceremony began, Coop took her hand and faced the minister as they spoke their promises to one another.

She was where she belonged, with Coop and their expanded family. She was doing the work of her heart's desire. With the help of Blake Charles, she was now the owner of a one-of-a-kind bridal salon, previously known as the Purple

Pansy, on the corner of Bluebonnet and Laurel newly named Promises by Taylor.

But mostly, and more importantly, she was the proud *owner* of Coop's loving heart.

The End

If you enjoyed this book, please leave a review at your favorite online retailer! Even if it's just a sentence or two it makes all the difference.

Thanks for reading *One-of-a-Kind Bride* by Charlene Sands!

Discover your next romance at TulePublishing.com.

More books by Charlene Sands

The Forever Texan series

Book 1: *Taming the Texas Cowboy*

Book 2: *Loving the Texas Lawman*

Book 3: *Redeeming the Texas Rancher*

Available now at your favorite online retailer!

About the Author

Charlene Sands is a USA Today Bestselling author writing sexy contemporary romances and stories set in the Old West. Her stories have been honored with the National Readers Choice Award, the Cataromance Reviewer's Choice Award and she's a double recipient of the Booksellers' Best Award. She was recently honored with Romantic Times Magazine's Best Harlequin Desire of 2014. Charlene is a member of the Orange County Chapter and Los Angeles Chapter of Romance Writers of America.

When not writing, she enjoys great coffee, spending time with her four "princesses", bowling in a woman's league, country music, reading books from her favorite authors and going on movie dates with her "hero" husband.

Thank you for reading

One-of-a-Kind Bride

If you enjoyed this book, you can find more from all our great authors at TulePublishing.com, or from your favorite online retailer.

Made in the USA
Middletown, DE
10 November 2021